A Perfect Disharmony

Sébastien Brebel

A PERFECT
DISHARMONY

STORIES

Translated from the French by Jesse Anderson

DALKEY ARCHIVE PRESS

Despite its mission to support French literature in translation, and in particular to support the cause and well-being of translators, CNL (Centre national du livre) would not provide support for the translator of this book, and this at a time when there has been a substantial decrease in the number of books being translated into English. Dalkey Archive urges CNL to return to its mission of aiding translators.

Originally published in French by P.O.L. as *La Baie vitree* in 2013.

Library of Congress Cataloging-in-Publication Data
Names: Brebel, Sāebastien, author. | Anderson, Jesse, 1987- translator.
Title: A perfect disharmony / by Sebastien Brebel ; stories translated by Jesse Anderson.
Description: First Dalkey Archive edition, 2017. | Victoria, TX : Dalkey Archive Press, 2017.
Identifiers: LCCN 2017006156 | ISBN 9781943150281 (pbk. : alk. paper)
Subjects: LCSH: Brebel, Sāebastien--Translations into English. | Short stories.
Classification: LCC PQ2702.R42 A2 2017 | DDC 843/.92--dc23
LC record available at https://lccn.loc.gov/2017006156/

www.dalkeyarchive.com
Victoria, TX / McLean, IL / Dublin

Dalkey Archive Press publications are, in part, made possible through the support of the University of Houston-Victoria and its programs in creative writing, publishing, and translation.

Printed on permanent/durable acid-free paper.

Contradiction

"I DON'T KNOW who you are."

And besides I wouldn't have the foolish pretension to try and get to know you, I'm irresistibly attracted to you and that's enough to make me happy, from the moment I saw you hanging from the arm of another I felt like some pathetic widower and lost any sense of self-worth, you're delightful and unpredictable, you're never unsure about yourself and I accept your decisions silently, though you express yourself clearly and effortlessly your simplest arguments are lost on me and when I listen to you speak I feel as if your words project flaming rays onto my hands, your motivations are obscure and your naked body intimidates me, your manners are medieval and your face is an enigma that lies beyond my comprehension, I desire you so much that I sometimes feel ashamed when I look at you and when you reject my advances I experience a sensation of sacred terror, I've renounced the use of my intelligence and can no longer think for myself, you often ask me to repeat a word under the pretext that I've mispronounced it and since I've known you my elocution has become hesitant and the sentences I address to you break down before I can complete them, I admire your casualness and your mistrust of conventions, I'd love to make some kind of impression on you but I tremble in your presence, I love you infinitely and foolishly and I feel guilty when I touch you, I fear for your life and am concerned for your well-being, I know that I can never truly satisfy you but your presence alone justifies the

3

sum of sacrifices and torments that I impose upon myself each day so that you never feel deprived of the things you desire, I monitor your diet and look for meaning in the smallest of your actions, I would love for you to stay slender and well-toned for the rest of your life, your silences kill me and your smile is like an iron rod swung straight into my bowels, you often prove to be brutal and unfair, even with our children whom you lost all interest in the moment they learned to say mama, I want to help you chase the dark thoughts from your mind but I express myself so poorly that there'd be no point in even trying, my attempts at attracting your attention are laughable and I never begin them without first dreading the embarrassment they might end in, I blame myself silently for my lack of tact and punish myself physically the moment you turn your back, I accumulate mountains of debt buying you clothes that might raise my merit in your eyes, I'm terrified you'll die of cancer and every time you come home late I assume you've ended your life for the sole purpose of making me suffer, your body is flexible and obeys you like a machine, your laugh is harsh and your hands are always cold, you're never out of breath although you smoke more than twenty cigarettes a day, every morning my waking thoughts are of you, I wonder what miracle brought you into my life and my struggles mean nothing beside the infinite joy I get from contemplating the body you so often conceal from me, my only fear is losing you, I can't stand us being in different rooms and when you shut yourself away in silence my heart begins to beat unsteadily, you look like some supernatural landscape and my only purpose in this world consists of loving you without any expectation of reciprocation, I'm grateful every day for the lucky fact that you were born, I'm never at peace in your presence, and to be perfectly honest, I sometimes feel like I've never actually met you.

But know as well that I see straight through your little games and can read your thoughts like a book whose pages

disintegrate as I carelessly flip through them, I can see the birth
of your emotions like a neurosurgeon watching the progression
of a brain tumor on some sophisticated machine, I know the
secrets of every square inch of your body which I cover as I
please with my sperm and saliva, you're completely passive and
I reign as master over your life, when I demand you to take off
your clothes you obey my instructions like a submissive child,
your limbs are like the detachable parts of a human-sized doll
that I manipulate according to my will, I bombard you with
hateful questions until you've fallen deep into sleep, I mock
your emotions and insult your friends and family when they
call to inquire about your health, I am the Grand Inquisitor
surging forth out of the depths of your soul to whisper
venomous words into your ear, I'm the architect of the horror-
filled cities you visit in your dreams, you drink up my words
like a disciple, you're completely transparent in everything you
do and I see through your thin skin like cigarette paper, I am
the embodiment of truth, my scientific and intellectual powers
are limitless, I'm the origin of your decisions and the factory
of your desires, I can divine your emotions and toothaches, I
see your fantasies the moment they take shape in your head
and I can tell by your body odor whether you're satisfied or
upset, I obsessively direct the path of your panicked blood as
it flows through your veins and I control the beating of your
heart, I see through all your moods and actions, I can make you
come in less than a minute and I force you to pose obscenely
for photographs, I have the power to make morbid thoughts
appear in your mind which keep you on edge for weeks at a
time, I love to forcibly and violently cut your hair without any
regard for your comfort, from the moment I saw you I knew
you were made for me, whenever I'm in the same room as you
I'm blinded by desire and my stomach feels as light as it was on
our first date together, although you're completely uninventive
in bed I never tire of making love to you, you're simple and

painfully predictable and your efforts at surprising me always end in failure, your aloofness bores me and your sentimentality annoys me, the banality of your ideas is pathetic and when you cry I want to hit you, you mean nothing to me, your actions leave no trace on my memory and I laugh to myself at your schemes to try and charm me, we exist together in a perfect disharmony, every Sunday you endure my hatred and laziness in an apartment that is far too small and far too damp, I rant against the overly salted meals you serve me with the timidity of an abused housewife and you recite to me a list of my mistresses while we eat, you make no complaints against my moodiness and I've persuaded you to spend the most beautiful hours of your existence at my side, you rarely speak in my presence out of fear that I'll criticize you and the affected complexity of your sentences gives me a headache, I regularly criticize you for your poor taste in clothing and I force you to wear skirts so short that they attract the predatory stares of men in the street, someday I'll leave you without even realizing it and the men you'll see afterwards will be nothing more than hollow corpses that pile up over the remainder of your life, I've known the children we'll never have together without taking any interest in their futures, I meet your eyes every day on the 6:07 train and every time you smile at me you seem so banal and so pathetic that I doubt if you even exist.

The Picture Window

SHE LIVES IN a villa facing the ocean, and she's expected at a funeral. She wears an elegantly cut black dress and holds a purse in her hand. She's young and urbane. She's lonely and prone to depression. She's situated herself near the picture window. Her body is thin, her facial features are precise. The entirety of her presence expresses a tired sobriety that seems resistant to time. She doesn't feel sad, and at times she smiles without knowing why. She never asks herself if she's happy; she doesn't imagine that another life, successful and promising and filled with its own set of problems and satisfactions, awaits her elsewhere. The house has four floors and contains numerous rooms, all more or less in good shape, but its universe has been progressively reduced to the dimensions of the reception room on the ground floor. The room is spacious and bright, so large that the furniture within it seems abnormally small, like the furniture from a dollhouse. And she herself appears small as well, lost in the immensity. Aside from its unusual dimensions, the room offers the advantage of always being a comfortable temperature. In both summer and winter, she can walk through it wearing a nightgown, or even nothing at all, like she could in a hotel room. The floor is made of large oak boards that are rough to the touch. A long time has passed since she's noticed the scratches and dead insects that cover it. The walls are red; no paintings adorn them. The ceiling beams are the color of soot. At the other end of the room, opposite the picture window, she's put a partition up behind which lies a bed. She sleeps there every night wrapped

7

in a green velvet coat. Sometimes she sleeps more than fourteen consecutive hours without the slightest trace of a dream. She wakes up naturally, with the first light of day, and gets out of bed without any visible effort. She takes several steps around the room barefoot while rubbing her eyes, and then goes instinctively toward the picture window. She does things slowly and sometimes gives off the impression of trying to limit the number of her movements. Her days unfold identically down to the smallest details, her routine has been perfected by repetition and a form of resignation derived from her inactivity. She's never disturbed by visitors and does nothing to entertain herself. She's attentive and collected, as if at the threshold of a new, slightly abstract existence, one removed from the uncertainties of time. She never tires of watching the ocean through the picture window. The sea is usually calm, slightly gray; it rarely seems threatening. The waves come to die softly some ten meters from the terrace. The beach is free of rocks, the horizon empty. She feels no anxiety when thinking about the future, she doesn't concern herself with thoughts of possible catastrophe. On rare occasions, the ocean will rise above its normal level, the water still calm, and climb several inches above the bottom of the picture window; when this happens, she moves closer to the window and watches the fish and particles floating in the water as if through an aquarium. The house is completely waterproofed, and she feels secure inside of it. On sunny days, she spreads out a sleeping bag alongside the picture window. She lies as close to the window as possible, her arms stretched out along her body, her palms turned toward the sky. Then she closes her eyes. A warm and irresistible laziness paralyzes her. With her body warmed by the sun's rays, she watches the waves as if inside a dream. During these moments, the other rooms of the house seem cold and dark, filled with hostile objects and enemy presences. She refuses to go up to the higher floors, out of fear of spraining an ankle on the stairs or stumbling upon an intruder.

Without feeling nostalgic, she can make a mental inventory of her personal belongings stored throughout the house: a pair of timeless leather boots, a dress she was once especially fond of, a sea green nightgown she wore during a hospital stay, books whose titles she's forgotten. The house's noises don't bother her; like the scratches on the floor or the wrinkles on her hands, they've become a part of her life. She's never bored, although she rarely has the feeling of being occupied or focused on something. She doesn't take care of the house, she neglects doing any chores. She can't remember having done the dishes a single time since she's been here. Everyday concerns make brief incursions into her thoughts but then tumble back down into a void of forgetfulness. Sometimes she puts on makeup for an imaginary appointment or date: she's invited out to dinner by a childhood friend who's been courting her for years and she reacts scathingly to any attempt on his part to be agreeable with her; she's summoned to a job interview during which a blond woman with long slender fingers looks her over with a thin smile; she stretches out on a table while trying to remember the date of her last sexual relationship. She's satisfied with her sedentary way of life, she harbors no dreams of traveling, and she can't remember having lived anywhere else. She never feels like she's trapped here and is never tempted to cross the threshold of the villa. She isn't sure if she can drive a car or find her way with a map, and she hates the idea of having to ask someone for directions. She remembers a time when there was a garden beyond the terrace, but she can't recall its precise layout or the plants that grew there or the hours she spent in it. She's lost her interest in the seasons, in trees and in rainbows, she doesn't think about how old she is. She remembers that when she arrived here there were other houses in the area, but she doesn't wonder what's become of their occupants. For the most part, she's uninterested in her past. She experiences no desire to express her thoughts or to be listened to. When she talks in her sleep, she says words whose strange beauty would astonish her. She rarely turns on the TV, and when she does, she watches with the sound muted, reading the actors' lips and trying to guess what they're thinking when their backs are turned to the camera. The alarm clock at the foot of the bed no longer works. When night comes, she stares at its green hands and imagines the subtle mechanisms of its indestructible cogs and springs until she seems to have worked her way into the clock's interior. Then she falls asleep, plunged into the darkness of the alarm clock, among the cogs and springs, safely sheltered in its copper matrix. In the morning, the clock becomes once again inoffensive. One day, in the middle of the afternoon, the sea withdrew further than usual, revealing a neatly cut portion of lawn in front of the house. With her forehead pressed to the window, she stared out at the trimmed grass until she made out a moving black dot, and then a second. The two united dots grew until they became two men's silhouettes, and after an indefinite amount of time, during which her eyes never left the men, she could at last make out two golfers, sometimes motionless, sometimes moving across the lawn with their golf bags dragging behind them. They were soon so close to the picture window that she could make out their pleated golf pants and plaid jackets, but she was still unable to guess their age or find any significance in their movements. The two men were beaming with laughter, and their attitude seemed to be a combination of insouciance and abruptness. She made a sign to them with her hand, but they pretended not to notice and went on laughing. When they were at last out of sight, she felt immense relief. The next morning, the ocean was back to its normal level. She got married at a very young age to a Swiss businessman. There are things she wishes she'd done that she couldn't do, things she did that she wishes she hadn't. Some time ago, she gave birth to three children. The eldest looks very much like her, he now studies in a foreign country. He's an anxious and brilliant boy who regularly sends her news of his life. He's sociable and passionate about the natural sciences and mathematics. He attends many conferences and publishes scholarly articles in specialist journals. He sends her long-winded letters, which dissipate her distress if she's feeling unhappy or neglected, that she never bothers responding to. Regarding the fact of their physical resemblance, she's always had trouble distinguishing his existence from her own, and despite the distance that separates them, she feels as if they live in the same neighborhood. She tells herself that if she were to die, he would die also, killed at the exact same instant thousands of kilometers away, in a high-speed car crash or from cardiac arrest or a ruptured aneurysm while riding on a tram. The second son leads a life so orderly and secretive that she can't help but distrust him. Every time she hears his voice on the phone, it takes her a moment to recognize it. She listens to him without comprehension, impatient for the conversation to come to an end. He's always spoken hesitantly and in grammatically incorrect sentences, as if trying to hide his true thoughts from her. She has difficulty remembering if the third child is a boy or a girl and would be unable to comment on the nature of their relationship. Out of either modesty or superstition, she rarely pronounces the names of her children. She forbids herself from thinking about them on their birthdays, she's destroyed all of their photos because they didn't look realistic to her. She isn't an affectionate person, and she's unmoved by compliments on her beauty or youthful appearance. Her name is either Emmanuelle or Elizabeth. Few things impress her, and she avoids conversations that would oblige her to argue. She sometimes tells herself that she lacks certain social abilities, that she should be more warmhearted, more communicative. When the telephone rings, she hesitates before answering, fearing that the caller will demand money or make unfounded accusations against her. One day when she didn't want to be disturbed, she wrapped the phone in an orange piece of cloth and tied it with cooking twine, imagining she could apply this method to cover everything surrounding her, the walls, the floor, the electric tubing, every single object, her clothes included. When she has trouble sleeping, she sits near the picture window and watches her reflection in the glass. She sees the face of a woman who resembles a bird, or a bird who resembles a woman, or both at the same time. This morning, the phone began ringing with a nearly insupportable insistence. After hanging it up, she spent the whole day seated on her bed, feeling dazed and watching the pastoral scenes on the partition until she was overcome by nausea. Finally, she got up with a kind of calculated deliberateness, took her purse from the shelf, and, after a moment of hesitation, went toward the picture window. An imposing shape now fills its frame: bristling with cannons, a destroyer has dropped anchor just in front of the villa. Its flags flutter in the wind like pennants at a fair, and she can see the sailors, dressed in fireproof uniforms, working on the bridge. The sun's rays reflect off the gray steel hull. She mechanically reads the name of the warship several times in a row, as if trying to decipher a price tag on the inside of a piece of clothing found in a trunk. She lives in a house facing the ocean, and she's expected at a funeral. Outside, parked on the side of the road, a black car is waiting for her. She lights a cigarette while contemplating the busy silhouettes on the bridge of the destroyer.

The Connection

SHE LIVES IN a green house on the edge of a river, and he's still unsure whether or not she lives there alone. Months can go by without him receiving news from her, months during which he seems to wander through a gray and lukewarm world made up of an endless boredom. He'd like to be able to forget her and go on with his life as if she never existed, but all his efforts to chase her from his thoughts only reinforce the grip she has on him. The first time she invited him to come to her house, she whispered an address he wasn't sure he understood, giving him directions so detailed and complex that he thought she might have been trying to lose him. Following her instructions, he walked through a series of streets while regularly checking behind him to make sure he wasn't being followed, then waited for nearly an hour at a bus station for his connection, keeping his face lowered to avoid being recognized. Overcome by reluctance after he'd boarded, he contemplated a barren and unfamiliar landscape through the window of the bus as if he'd suddenly found himself in a parallel world made up of strange trees, pylons, and tractors frozen in the mist. He was the last passenger to get off at the terminal station and he still had to circle through the streets of a deserted village, filled with dilapidated houses crumbling into each other, before walking along a country road on the edge of a riverbank that led out of town. Night had fallen when he finally found himself before the house. He hesitated before knocking, and after a long delay, she appeared through a crack in the door, wearing a silk bathrobe decorated with large, yellow flowers. She looked him over. The hand that she ran through his hair sent waves of excitement coursing through his body.

She calls him in the middle of the night under the unconvincing pretext that she saw him die horribly in a dream and wants to make sure he's still alive. It takes him a minute to recognize her voice. As if she were drunk or heavily medicated, she seems to be having difficulties expressing herself, or perhaps she simply wants to confuse or tease him. She talks to him about a trip she once made, thirty years earlier, during the course of which she contracted an infectious disease and purchased an indigenous mask whose potential value she's interested in having evaluated in order to sell it to an ethnographic museum. She talks to him about her white hair and her solitude. She talks about her soft hands that have never lovingly touched anyone. She recounts her day to him in detail, from the moment she first moved her legs upon waking to the morning light, to the moment she sank into sleep as if into a deep, dark pool of water. She describes her solitary walks through the forest and paints for him her emotions, which sound like they come from another planet. She confirms that she has always lived apart from other people and that he's the first person to show any interest in her. She thanks him for sparing her any confidences which she wouldn't know what to do with, and she's grateful that he's willing to not bring up the feelings he experiences for her. For the thousandth time, she forbids him from speaking about her to anyone and then, after making him swear that he won't come looking for her without written permission, violently hangs up. The next day, he finds himself doubting her existence, but at the memory of her bizarrely and excessively spread fingers, he realizes she must be real. He suspects her of lying, of plotting coldly against him. Sometimes she's demanding and assertive and orders him to carry out pointless tasks that she soon forgets and then scolds him for bringing up again. He helps her get her affairs in order, she dictates vindictive and venomous letters to him, written in red ink and addressed to a hypothetical disabled nephew with whom there is some issue of inheritance and betrayal. She makes an effort to educate him, to break down his conformity and erase his naïve attachment to commonly held values. She once claimed that he had a non-descript, interchangeable face, and that any first name would suit him, adding that she'd be more attracted to him if he had the facial features of a foreigner or a criminal. She accuses him of having had a sheltered upbringing that prevented him from developing a unique personality and having cowardly modeled himself after his melancholic father. She'd love to push him out of the city, away from the alienation of his job and the repetitive routines of his bachelorhood. She'd like to present him to vivacious, marginalized women, simpleminded but consenting, eager to satisfy his sexual needs the instant they form in his head and around whom he would eventually come to feel the intolerable boredom of public holidays. She'd like to make him permanently disgusted with sex and convince him to join a rifle club. She predicts that his life will unfold without depth or surprise, a progression of years as flat as a corpse's EKG. One day, without explanation, she offers him a velvet jacket whose sleeves are too short. He feels as if there's no limit to what she might demand from him and knows that he'd be willing to do anything to satisfy her.

For two whole years, he had no word from her and lived under the assumption that she'd ended her life, choosing not to tell him beforehand with the intention of convincing him of her immortality. Then, out of nowhere, he received a crumpled letter that must have spent months at the bottom of a pocket or purse and whose writing, seemingly deformed by excitement, was so violent and irregular that it took him hours to decipher. She told him to meet her in a hotel room, where she'd supposedly been living for some time, in a city he'd never heard of. Looking over the envelope, he thought he recognized postage from Madagascar or Tanzania before realizing that it was actually an illustration cut out of a magazine dedicated to stamp collecting. A week later, she showed up at his house as if it was perfectly normal and closely examined him from the soles of his feet to the top of his head before inspecting his skin with the careful attention of a dermatologist. As if she had inexplicably traveled back in time, she seemed younger and more innocent, and her softened features gave off the strange tranquility of a mental patient. She ignored all of his questions and spoke only of his bad taste, clearly demonstrated by the arrangement of his apartment.

She could be fifty years old, maybe more, yet she is young, frighteningly young, and everything about her is pure and fresh. He met her on a slightly rainy day, in a deserted cafeteria with orange carpeting. Seated one table away, she made an ambiguous motion in his direction, which he didn't at first understand was meant for him. When they were finally sitting face to face after a long hesitation, she turned her head away and acted entirely uninterested in him before a single word could be exchanged. He felt embarrassed and awkward, strangely attracted to her stubbornness and impropriety, and he hid his shaking hands beneath the table. She suggested that he come do some repair work at her house in exchange for a laughable sum of money, barely enough to buy a sweater or a carton of cigarettes. She insisted that he accept, staring at him with eyes that looked like green stones fallen from the sky. She ended the conversation by offering to pay for his coffee and inviting him to follow her through the city, which, once outside, seemed suddenly foreign and hostile, as if he hadn't set foot there in years. The sidewalks and the facades seemed to reject their presence, and several times he noticed the spiteful glances of other pedestrians. They let themselves get lost on the trails of a cemetery while she amused herself by reading the names written on the tombstones, then they settled themselves beneath the barren trees of an empty park, where a dog barked at their arrival. Walking through the city like two shadows, they never spoke. She left him suddenly at a crosswalk, instructing him to meet her in the same place the next day without bothering to mention at what time.

Her house is cramped and rises four stories into the sky. It's divided into tiny bedrooms with extremely low ceilings and is cluttered with trinkets, colored bottles, and spun-glass objects on display in cabinets. The house is dominated by a damp, oppressive warmth, an atmosphere like a greenhouse or an incubator. When she agrees to have him over, she puts him in a small, unheated room filled with brooms and pungent cleaning products, where he sleeps on a foldout bed with springs that stab into his sides. She forbids him from exploring the house alone and threatens to throw him out if he disobeys. She receives him in a nightgown no matter what time of day it is, and always tells him to remove his shoes before coming in. She offers him a glass of water and then, as if trying to provoke some reaction out of him, stands imposingly before him while he drinks. She interrogates him in a distracted and frustrated tone without listening to his responses. She speaks passionately and vehemently to him for hours and never offers him anything to eat. When she notices that he's getting bored, she begins to speak slowly in a voice close to tears, and he begins to feel the sprawling warmth of a trap closing in around him. She brags to him about the suppleness of her legs, the abundance of her hair, and the youthfulness of her figure. She becomes lustful, nasty, rambling. Her skin is firm but unusually white, and he would give anything in the world for a chance to explore its most hidden recesses. Hypnotized by her own suggestively pronounced words, she rambles on into the middle of the night, and after demanding that he undress in front of her, she rubs her fingers over his thighs and stomach and claims that his penis was designed for her mouth. She once made him promise that he would never allow himself to give weakly into the desire of ejaculating into another woman's body. One night when she'd been drinking, she gave him permission to hold her breasts but has since then accused him of being perverted and having taken advantage of her. He feels something close to happiness every time he leaves her and finds himself distraught, disgusted, and aimless, alone again in the street.

She criticizes his laziness and refuses his sexual advances. She can be simultaneously distant and provocative. She mocks his seriousness and his self-centered preoccupations. She suggests that he wear more elegant clothing and improve his body by working out. She takes showers throughout the day, showing a dedication to hygiene so demanding that he sometimes feels filthy in comparison, his clothes covered in stains, his body giving off unpleasant odors. She recommends him creams for treating psoriasis, taking advantage of his inborn hypochondria. She tells him that at his age she had a collection of lovers, slept less than five hours a night, and changed the color of her hair at least once a month. She goes to a swimming pool three times a week, performing laps like a swimming champion. She takes care of her body, her makeup takes hours to put on. She possesses the secret of eternal youth and a variety of formulas for avoiding destructive emotions. Her diet consists exclusively of red meat and cornichons, and she drinks a glass of whiskey every night before going to bed. At the age of five, she was put into an orphanage after her parents died in a plane crash over the territorial waters of Norway. She was raped by her uncle at the age of twelve, she defeated cancer at thirty-five, and since then she has never consulted a doctor. Death doesn't frighten her, but the subject of aging makes her nauseous. She is unaffected by exhaustion, fatigue, sickness, and decline, and she doesn't have to be angry to be threatening. She's unfaithful and endowed with a calm power of destruction that she demonstrates in tiny doses through her words and actions. When he tries to get her attention, hoping that she'll let him come a little closer to her, she looks in another direction and acts annoyed by his slight speech impediment. No happiness dwells within her, and a complete absence of pity has taken the place of her morality. A burst of bullets from a machine gun wouldn't knock her down, and she would prove resistant to any virus nature could come up with. One day, when she seemed bored or distracted, he begged her to show him a picture of herself when she was young and, overcome with rage, she flung a pornographic magazine in his direction, claiming that he'd find something inside to satisfy his disgusting curiosity. When she lets him kiss her behind the ears, the smell reminds him of nothing at all.

He has difficulty forming a precise image of her and, when he accepts that's he really even met her, believing that she could disappear from his life at any moment. He would love to be capable of hating her, or of at least finding her pathetic. At times he feels as if he's always known her, that she was with him from his first day on Earth, disguised as a nurse's aide in the hospital corridor, waiting for the right moment to lean over his cradle and whisper ruinous words into his ear. In a recurring nightmare he had in the months leading up to his sixth birthday, she took on the face of a drowning woman who tried to grab him and drag him down with her into the freezing waters of a mountain lake. She was always lurking somewhere behind him in the years that followed, monitoring his development and obsessively haunting his existence, hovering in the background like a repressed anxiety or an unfavorable omen. She's made him lose interest in living by infecting him with a repulsion to anything that isn't her face, her body, or her voice. He feels a senseless longing for her to which she remains deaf. He leaves his house less and less often, his friends avoid him, and the women who meet his eyes in the street stare at him as if he were suffering from some disgraceful disease. He's never felt so weak and so strong, and on certain nights as he lays down for bed, he seriously considers putting an end to his detestable and hollow existence.

Metamorphosis

SHE SITS SILENTLY on a bench while on her face emotions take shape and fade at nearly the speed of light. She's wearing a crumpled, gray raincoat, her eyes are bright, unnaturally so. She's thin and composed, her fingers are curled into a half-formed fist, her large, protruding forehead suggests a childish stubbornness. Slightly hunched over as if reading a letter set on her knees, she's positioned herself to avoid meeting the eyes of the people passing by, fearing that she might be recognized. She sometimes lifts her head in the direction of the double casement windows of a house across the street. She imagines the bourgeois interior, kept clean and tidy by inactive housewives who keep their boredom at bay by flipping through fashion magazines. The sound of a piano escaping from a living room brings to mind memories of her childhood, which she's sure to destroy the second they form in her head. She's been sitting here now for several days, as immobile and calm as a statue on Easter Island. She has the aura of a femme fatale, a child, a survivor of some natural disaster. She doesn't appear fragile, she doesn't inspire pity. Around her body, the air circulates with the rhythm of her slow, regular breaths, which are themselves synchronized to the beating of her athletic heart. She never puts on makeup, and she wears flat-heeled shoes. She can't stand the soft texture of carpets, preferring the antiseptic chill of tiles. She dreams of a house that she can die in, made up of hallways without doors and rooms without windows. She would take her time visiting each room individually, walking barefoot and bumping into the furniture as if in a dream, stumbling through the darkness in the hope of finding her own body rolled up into a rug. Multiple times in her life she's been propositioned by men to sleep with them in exchange for money. The first time she said she wanted to keep her virginity until marriage, but she doesn't remember ever having refused in the times that followed, at first because of how easy the money was and then out of a kind of refined habit which earned her a coworker's admiration when, in an effort to satisfy a need as artificial as it was fleeting for complicity, she let her in on this secret after drinking too much one night in a small, deserted Chinese restaurant. She keeps to herself, she requires nothing. She could be content anywhere, in a seedy hotel room with flower wallpaper, in the waiting room of a gynecologist, or in an airport concourse among a crowd of nervous passengers listening to an announcement of imminent disaster. An unbridgeable distance would always exist between her and other people. As a little girl, she spent her vacations in a lake house where she was often bored and whose walls and ceilings, bare and painted white, displayed the prodigious remains of insects smashed by her hysteric father. When her parents told her they were getting a divorce, visibly relieved by a decision that had taken more than twenty years to make due to concerns that a hasty separation would bankrupt the modest capital years of work and savings had allowed them to accumulate, she took the news lightly and received a shower of castigation in return. She'd allegedly ruined their relationship, keeping a constant and perverse surveillance over their lives since her earliest years. She'd unrelentingly judged them and had regularly pointed out their most inconsequential shortcomings, they'd even found microphones hidden throughout their bedroom but, fearing she would unleash an unthinkable revenge on them, had decided to not bring it up. At twenty-eight years old, she'd learned how to keep her fears stored away in a secure place. Her worst memories are mixed with perfectly inoffensive images from her childhood and her most hateful thoughts fertilize the arid fields of her future. Unacquainted with the nature of happiness, she uses a convincing positivity to deceive others of her mood. She has the feeling of never having spoken with someone worthy of her conversation and of having amassed a collection of misunderstandings. Her handwriting is careful and consistent and reveals a great mastery of self. She's filled whole pages of her notebook with perfectly rendered pictures of miniature gallows. She's resisted the temptations of both drugs and forbidden fruit. She's magnificent and miserable. She experiences a pain whose source exists outside of her mind or body, an ancient and elusive pain that comes from a time before she or her parents were born. She's convinced that she'll get fatter as she grows older and that her face will undergo an unstoppable thickening as the years go by, overrun by a plaster of flesh that will eventually hide the natural delicacy of her features. At unexpected moments, she senses that her end is near and that a swift death is preparing itself to snatch her away. She dreams of being a wealthy heiress stretched out on a chaise longue beside a swimming pool, deprived of the use of her arms and legs, nourished with the help of a tube. She could have been a normal young mother, one who leans over two small identical beds to kiss her children goodnight, a leisurely woman living in an elegantly decorated house in the countryside. The hum of the cars on a nearby road would have made up the soundtrack of her days, offering a companionship more satisfying and reassuring than the empty words and unwanted advances of a man. The well-tended garden would have reflected a sensitive demeanor and an acute sense of symmetry. Seated near the end of the morning at the table of an impeccably equipped kitchen, admiring the cleanliness of the windows and watching the reflections of light on the blades of the knives and the handles of cupboards, she would have experienced an ideal form of boredom, cleansed of any discordant notes. The next day, she would be briefly mentioned in the local newspaper's crime section for the murder of two seven-month-old infants. People would pity her family, and her husband would testify, holding back tears, on a popular TV show. No one is ever sure of her age, or her youth, or her maturity. No one is ever really sure who she is at all. One wonders if she's ever truly felt human emotions. A photo of her shows a smiling child with a boy's haircut, posing in front of a field of sunflowers that forms a dense and ominous forest around her. Her face shows an almost imperceptible anxiety, which is emphasized by the black hearts of the flowers turned toward the camera. A second photo shows her from a low-angle shot: eyes half-closed and hair falling freely onto naked shoulders, it was likely taken by a former lover just after a shower. In a third, she stands beside Hitler on the Berghof's terrace. She's never been in love. When she was fourteen, she exchanged kisses and touches with another girl on a hospital bed. Signs of potential seizures and concealed scars seem to appear and disappear rapidly on her face. She arouses aggression in women close to her age and has an immediate erotic impact on men. She was once proposed to by a neurosurgeon and gave herself two hours later to a medical student in a wheelchair who'd asked her for the time. She's never deigned to respond to the heartrending letters sent from abroad by her brother, judging them to be as poorly written as they are obscene. She owns an autographed copy of a Philip Roth novel and once maintained a brief and tormented relationship with Turgenev. Sometimes a passerby stops, approaches her slowly, and in a gesture of hesitant compassion, offers her a hot croissant or a condom. This morning, a malnourished teenager, wearing a T-shirt stained with white sauce, came up to her and asked her if she was a whore. She's made a resolution to never interfere in someone else's life. She once screamed at her neighbors the second she could hear them whispering through the paper-thin wall separating their living rooms. Her apartment has begun to stink, torn envelopes and credit card receipts are strewn about the dark red carpet, trans-

forming the area around her bed into a polluted riverbank. The
last time she was there, she put on a raincoat and slammed the
door behind her, and when she realized that she'd left her keys
inside, an ecstatic smile, which revealed a profound sadness, illuminated her face. Penniless, she walked through the streets for
an indefinite amount of time. At some point, a concierge chased
her on foot after she'd relieved herself in the entranceway of a
building, spilling abundant amounts of urine into the cracks of
the cobblestone. Her head buzzing with excitement, she started
toward the train station, where, without taking the time to
check its destination, she rushed onto the first available train.

She agrees to come with me to the apartment I've been renting
for several weeks in an old building with a blackened façade, two
streets from where we meet. Now that she's at my side, she seems
smaller, simpler even, than when she was sitting on the bench.
In the cramped elevator taking us toward the fifth floor, she lifts
the collar of her jacket up to her chin and smiles lightly at me
with a disturbing bluntness that is both tired and mocking. She
watches me with an indifference nuanced with disdain, showing
no sign of distrust or surprise. She goes into the living room and,
without my invitation, sits in the first chair she finds. She pays
no attention to the unpacked boxes or the titles of the books
on my shelves. She still seems somewhat shy and curt, but she
confidently meets my eyes when I tell her to make herself at
home. She has the attitude of a delinquent cashier or a failed
actress. A decisive tension subtly animates her movements and
impregnates her silence. She doesn't touch the hot cup of tea I
set before her on the small living room table and is satisfied to
simply suck on the two cubes of sugar sitting on the edge of
the saucer. She lets me sit with her until nightfall, responding
to my questions with a hostile reluctance, then stands up and
walks toward the bedroom, staring expectantly in my direction.
She finally agrees to take a shower the following morning, after

commanding me to leave the apartment for fifteen minutes. Standing on the sidewalk across from my building, I keep the entryway in sight, afraid that she might try to escape, taking advantage of my absence to lay waste to my apartment or to set my mattress on fire. When I come back, she smiles at me with a touch of silent reproach, as if she was mad at me for abandoning her, but then puts up no resistance to my advances. She's usually silent and unexpressive, as if she were extremely focused on what was going on inside herself. She responds to my questions with a yes or a no and is unresponsive to my attempts to coax her into talking. Unperturbed by the air of impoverishment they lend her appearance, she agrees to wear the cheapest dresses I can find at the neighborhood supermarket. She lives off cookies and never turns on the TV without asking for my permission. She's distrustful of comfort and laughs at my plans for renovation. Her plans for the future consist entirely of a ski trip that I vaguely promised her in exchange for a kiss, which she'd until then refused me. She knows how to serve herself with a fork and she wields a broom with ease. Like a hunted animal, her senses are always on alert, and her education seems to be riddled with omissions and holes. She regularly forgets to close the refrigerator door and balks at the idea of changing her underwear on a daily basis. Her frequent errors in pronunciation are painful to my ears and make me feel as if I'm living with a five-year-old. On my bedroom wall, she's hung up collages made from photos of my parents, whose frozen poses she compliments sarcastically. When I come home from work, she looks at me with surprise and terror, as if it were the first time she's ever seen me and is expecting a violent reaction out of me. I take her head in my hands, place my lips on her cool cheek, and receive an icy look in return. Due to either laziness or lack of interest, she refuses to accompany me to the movies, and she systematically declines my offers to take her to the beach, claiming that exposure to the sun causes her skin to break out in disgusting marks that take months to fade. To escape my boredom and solitude, I take long, invigorating baths, pretending that my limbs are mechanical oars which I use to push myself further and further away from the beach, moving at a consistent, even speed, until the children's screams become inaudible, as muddled and blurred as the fine strokes of color on a pointillist painting. When I'm out in the street, I seem to see her several times a day, sometimes even following her into grocery stores or libraries, staying with her until the moment I'm about to approach and then, at the last second with my heart racing, realize my mistake. She inspires in me ideas for horror films and her freckle-covered body has the sour taste of my nocturnal terrors. She uses red ink to correct the spelling mistakes on my manuscripts, and she criticizes the sluggishness of my writing style. She regularly cuts off locks from my hair, which she then disposes of in the toilet bowl. At night, she explodes out of the sheets, naked and white, to cut short the telephone's intrusive ringing. She never clears the table and leaves her clothes scattered throughout the apartment. She struts around in tiny pink panties from morning to evening, indifferent to the stares of the residents in the building across the street. Every night before going to bed, she massages a beauty cream into her breasts, thighs, and ass cheeks, then, as if to dissuade me from touching her, lays down with an infinite number of precautions, her arms extended along her body, the palms placed flat on the mattress, the fingers spaced slightly apart, in a position that's claimed to encourage cellular regeneration. Upon waking, her dry, raspy voice pronounces words that sound as rough as the rubbing of emery cloth. From her pupils to her ankles, she seems to have been created to seduce me. Her hygiene is wanting, her thinness sometimes terrifies me, I've given up on trying to find the reasons I'm so attracted to her. When she talks with her mouth full, bits of food cover my arms and I have to leave the room to stop myself from hitting her. She never asks for favors, but she makes no sacrifices to make my life more pleasant. I've become jealous, pathologically so, although I know she's incapable of crossing the threshold of the apartment. Her rare words, spoken in a voice weighted down by the anxiolytics she swallows without moderation, confuse me and lull my vigilance. She's slow but agile, her black hair coils around her body like the deeply engrained connections that keep her captive to her nightmares. When I try to be tender with her, her features harden and freeze like a statue's. I don't let her out of my sight, I dream of her every night, I let myself succumb to her presence to a point of stupefaction. She swings unpredictably between fright and joy, between indifference and passion, and my fate is to love her without knowing why. I can no longer live without her silent presence, her sudden mood changes, the sickly sweet odor exhaled by her body. I know nothing about her background, the motives behind her behavior escape me, and I suspect she hasn't told me her real name. With her eyes opened wide, she swallows my sperm like a submissive student, taking it in like an antibiotic or a health food with a widely recognized nutritional value. I am never gentle with her. My hands rub her breasts, my fingers search her vulva, her anus, I accost her body for hours at a time. Eventually, she'll develop the attitude of an overfed princess and demand that I bring her new lovers on a silver platter. She'll forbid me from entering her room, and I'll plead with her to let me see her breasts one final time before I disappear forever, and one April morning, after driving for hours in a state of impotent rage and frustration, I'll throw myself off a cliff. She won't notice my absence and, glued in front of the TV, will quickly exhaust her reserves of food. One night, she'll transform into a white rabbit, so fat and so enormous that the bars of her cage will dig painfully into her flesh.

Antonia

"OPEN YOUR EYES wide, this is the last time you'll see me."

She lives in a two-room apartment with her mentally ill mother and claims to possess little more than her misery and her bouts of insomnia. It's been months since she's took any initiative or checked the mail, and on some mornings, it takes her more than three hours to get out of bed. She's never been a big eater, and she usually drinks a glass of lukewarm tap water in place of breakfast. She has a sensation of suffocating between the four walls of her isolated existence, and her days are like endless tunnels whose distance she tries to shorten by gnawing at her fingernails. As if in preparation for a date with herself, during which she intends to both astonish and seduce, she changes her outfits and hairstyle several times per day. She listens to the radio for hours on end, the volume turned to its lowest level to give her the impression of eavesdropping on a secret meeting. She listens to political speeches that sound like forgotten operettas and weather reports that predict hurricanes and tornados in a barely audible voice. She doesn't smoke and drinks only with reluctance, emptying her glass in quick mouthfuls before carefully running her tongue over her lips to get rid of the bitter taste. She feeds herself sparingly and sometimes, as if taking a vacation from her body's needs, goes long stretches without feeling any desire to eat. She's often tempted to go out but is overwhelmed by panic the moment she's alone in public. There's no place for either surprise or irony in her life, and she neglects the thousands and thousands of expected formalities that swarm around every social interaction and give meaning to the most mundane of human relationships. It's never made sense to her to try and progress in a world so poorly designed for her that she's unsure of ever having known the correct way to maneuver her arms, legs, or hands. Sitting at a café terrace, she feels x-rayed by the hostile glances directed her way, and after five minutes, the noise and conversation surrounding her begin to feel like torture. Since her twenty-first birthday, she's suffered from a chronic arrhythmia. She bought a stethoscope through the mail and, stretched out on the floor, often listens to the beating of her heart, monitoring the abnormality she's come to think of as a well-deserved punishment. Some days, without knowing why, she feels overcome by ambition, ready to trade her mediocre life for the smallest possibility of change, until the moment she hears the hate-filled voice of her mother screaming in defiance at the brightness of the morning.

"I don't have much time, you know. My mother could wake up at any moment."

Because her mother stays in bed for the duration of the day, she alone is responsible for the apartment's upkeep and provisioning. One time per week, she searches through the aisles of a supermarket, pulling cans and premade meals off the shelves at random, overwhelmed by a fear that she'll find the apartment torn apart when she gets back. When she comes home from the corner laundromat, she remains silent as her mother insults her for leaving her home alone, threatening to call a lawyer to have her arraigned for failing to properly care for a person in need. She never has the energy to respond to her provocations and satisfies herself by drowning her thoughts in an opaque and solid form of hopelessness. In the streets, she walks with the same rhythm as the other pedestrians to prevent herself from being noticed. Although she usually seems absent from herself, she's never caught off guard. She has no memory of the day her father abandoned her and her mother at a highway rest stop on one of the hottest days of the summer, when she was three years old and suffering from eczema. She was six years old when she was almost kidnapped on her way to school by a man who changed his mind the instant he felt her cold, dry hand come into contact with his own. On the insistence of her mother, who suspected her teachers of inappropriately fondling her, she was forced to change her primary school three years in a row. Afraid of being abandoned by her ungrateful daughter, her mother forbids her from closing the door between the living room and her bedroom, and she often bursts into the bathroom at the most inappropriate times. She summons her almost every night to her bedside and, seizing her painfully by the wrist, begins to describe incoherent and horrible dreams, as if in an attempt to contaminate her imagination. During meals, she throws herself onto her plate like a famine victim, greedily devouring her food while staining the tablecloth and her clothes, then moves immediately to the TV without offering to help clean up. Her hatred for the world, stubborn and all-encompassing, finds distraction only in her fading passion for angels. Plunged into a state of misery and despondency during her deepest periods of depression, she'll spend hours playing an electric organ and singing ritornellos of some unknown, mystic origin.

"You don't want me, is that it? You don't like me because I'm too skinny?"

She wears a sequined dress and blows her nose loudly. Circles surround her eyes like artificial lakes, and she looks like she just came out of a nightclub or some parallel universe. She's pathetic and entrancing; she's vulnerable and vehement. Her eyes are golden, and the incurable sadness of her smile seems to have been spawned from the icy depths of unknown places. There's something both immaculate and indecent about her presence. She lists off her sorrows in a quiet, monotone voice, as if she were being held prisoner in a room filled with microphones. She doesn't finish her sentences, and she pronounces certain words as if she didn't understand their meaning. She warns me not to make any noise and to behave as if I was being hunted. She spends hours monitoring my comings and goings, her ear strained, turning in circles like a madwoman trapped in a waiting room from which there's no possibility of escape. Sometimes, under the power of some sudden impulse, she gets up in the middle of the night and situates herself at the bedroom window to watch the fragmented squares of light on the façade of the building across the street. She acts as spectator to the banal scenes of the building's tenants, mute actors with unexpressive faces who look as if they were being filmed in slow motion. The lights go on and off at irregular intervals, punctuating the façade like blinking lights on the dashboard of a phantom spaceship. One night, when all the lights were out, a sense of omnipotence took hold of her and she felt, climbing the length of her naked legs, the complicit touch of the moist and sticky earth beneath her feet. She places no more significance on the meaning of her dreams than she does on the decaying pieces of hair stuck to her bathtub's enamel. Her thoughts mature and decay according to the will of the fleeting sensations that form inside her head and teleport her to the furthest edges of the universe. The flight path of a fly can catapult her to the pyramids, a tingling in the tips of her fingers submerses her beneath the ice caps. The most physically demanding professions don't frighten her, she could acclimate herself to the most extreme temperatures and vanquish the pestilent heat of the apocalypse. She believes herself to be resistant to all disease and would fight for the abolition of vaccines if she had the ability to enter into contact with the outside world. Each morning, sheltered in her sleeping bag, she sinks her fingers into her vagina while imagining torrential rains blackening the sky. Water would rise to the level of her window and, as if on a small boat being rocked back and forth on a river current, she would barely have to stretch out her arm to dip in her fingers. She comes back every morning and says to me:

"I haven't taken anything, I'm not on any drugs. I wouldn't lie about something like that."

She shows no signs of frailty. At twenty-six years old, her face reveals a mysterious and calm maturity. She has no wrinkles, and she never sits with her legs crossed. She's secretly convinced of being immortal and believes that her perpetual boredom is a sign of royal heritage. She's made hurried love to strangers in phone booths and in the compartments of trains stopped at a marshalling yard. She moves seamlessly from enthusiasm to apathy, from fear to boredom. With eyes wide open, she'll dream out loud about conspiracies, murders, and orgies arranged by the office workers who meet once a month on her building's highest floor. Her body is indecent and flawed, like a face struck by the passage of years. She mocks me for my modesty and the red marks on my legs. She stares with a kind of undetermined insistence at the unmade sheets on my bed, then lets the matter go as if she were suddenly exhausted with it. She removes her clothes with a theatrical exaggeration, and when she finally stands before me completely naked, her arms outstretched like a sleepwalker or a drowned cadaver, I can't help but feel ashamed, as if it was me being exposed by her nudity.

"My name is Antonia. You don't know me, but don't be afraid. Do you mind if I come in for a minute?"

She's stopped coming to see me, and I whisper her name as if in a perfectly silent and hopelessly dreary dream, not a dream of my own but one which she's lured me into, motioning to me from behind a parlor window, speaking so softly that I have to follow the movement of her lips to understand her.

Melancholy

YOU CHARM ME, your presence electrifies me, I can't live without you. It took me three months to work up the courage to approach you, and when I talk to you, my attention falls immediately on your fingernails. You're like a magnet for my eyes, and not seeing you borders on the painful. I was first attracted to your hair, then to the delicate structure of your body, and the day I noticed the tiny scar on your right kneecap was the first time in my life that I knew what ecstasy truly was. You eat in silence with a drudging slowness, letting your saliva slowly soak the food before it slides down into your esophagus. I imagined how you might act while making love and thought up an infinite number of ways with which you might pleasure me. Your comforting face accelerates the beating of my heart, and your grandiloquence makes me cower. You're both provocative and vulgar. You claim to be a homebody and refuse to pick favorites from the adoring people who hover around you like drunken planets on an erratic orbit. I've never seen you blush, I've never seen the hair stand up on your arms. I can sense your annoyance when you're taken by surprise or feel in anyway threatened. You inspire me, I know almost nothing about you, and I'm close to being convinced that you're the source of all my fears. I could never criticize you, and every time I sense your behavior pushing me away, I find myself striving to tear down the psychic barriers that prevent me from fully understanding you. You never tire of the unending cycle of pointless get-togethers with friends and family, and you refuse to apologize when you show up late to our dates. You're voluble, instinctive, full of energy. You're invulnerable to both shame and regret, and you never show gratitude. You're unaware of your multitude of gifts, squandered on trivial and short-lived endeavors, and the origin of your decisions is a mystery I could never grow tired of contemplating. Your existence is a miracle. You've cast a spell on me, I can hardly believe I was able to live before I met you, and I won't rest until I've proven my potential to you with the help of small lies and exaggerations that fill me with an awareness of my own worthlessness. To keep myself occupied, I've spent six months making an folding partition based on a photo I stole from you, in which you sit naked, probably high on something, in a bathtub filled with soapy water. Although you're always sober when I'm around you, as if it were a point of honor to demonstrate your responsibility to me, your consumption of drugs is regular and discreet. I experience a morose delight when I listen to you talk about things I don't understand, feeling as if I live tens of thousands of kilometers away from you and your preoccupations. When you mention the numerous setbacks and failures that have punctuated your mournful and luckless existence, your facial features twist into a cold and abstract excitement. You could ignore me, forget about me, or send me away forever, I would continue to rejoice at the spectacle of your life until I'm dead and buried.

One Sunday morning, after two years of patient and well-planned seduction, all your resistances would crumble and, as if under effects of some powerful painkiller, you would show up unannounced at my door, insisting: "I haven't taken anything, I'm not on any drugs." I'd invite you in, my heart beating so hard it would feel like it might burst, and you'd go straight into my bedroom and bury yourself under the sheets without a word of explanation. You'd sleep for fourteen hours straight, and the next day you'd go through the cupboards and closets as if you'd always lived here and were looking for something specific. In the days following your arrival, I'd be grateful to you for not trying to deceive me with regards to the sudden change of mind that drove you to me, sensing that any such attempt would only serve to damage my ego. In response to your silence and crying fits during the difficult moments of our relationship, I'd prevent myself from bringing up your past and would pretend to forget the insidious remarks you made regarding my opinions and bachelor-like habits. Out of curiosity or spite, you would agree to trade your marginal and dynamic life for the security of a steady relationship, lukewarm and devoid of true affection. After fifteen days of cohabitation, financial problems would start to rear their heads, and we would soon learn the boredom and uncertainty of an inactive, out-of-work couple. The gray roofs, the sounds of the city, everything would appear heavy and motionless to us, and the disgraceful sound of our voices would reveal, from our first waking moments, our unrelenting exhaustion. Two months later, after stumbling little by little in the direction of each other's bodies and accumulating a large collection of indirect sexual allusions, we would sanctify our relationship by making love on the living room sofa. This first attempt, carried out like a chore, would be brief, intense, and disappointing, and would give us both a feeling of having destroyed any erotic potential in our relationship. Although money wouldn't interest you, I'd still take out a life insurance policy in anticipation of the day when, grateful for my corpse, you'd be able to cash in on the benefits. Out of self-hatred or fear that you might discover something distasteful in my personality, I would systematically seek out and destroy all traces of my past existence, burning the photos and letters that might reveal the mediocrity of the life I led before I met you. On the day of my parents' death, I'd be careful to hide the news from you and would go alone to the funeral, attending the ceremony in a sweat suit so as not to raise suspicion when I left the house. I'd struggle every day against the retrospective jealousy I'd feel when listening to the stories of your youthful adventures, and I'd become hateful and suspicious every time you brought up your past. You would frequently mention a brother who shuts himself away in a filthy bedroom and toward whom I would feel, without wondering why, an intense distrust. Your shamelessness would awake in me memories of childhood terrors. I'd design dresses for you that I would pay to have manufactured in a factory and which you'd only agree to wear while cleaning the house. I'd lovingly wash your hair every night, lighting little candles on the edge of the bathtub in homage to your beauty. I'd keep you jealously hidden away, like a stolen painting or a bottle of poison, and I would irrevocably break off all relations with my friends the day they made a comment revealing their limited appreciation of you. Our life would be reduced to an accumulation of days as smooth and white as enamel, and our matrimonial intimacy would consist solely of words exchanged between our respective corners of the living room, their main purpose being to verify that we were still alive. We'd rarely leave the house, preferring to do so only at the end of the day and mechanically going to the one park we knew of that could give us an illusion of living in an uninhabited city. We'd design the blueprints for an excessively complicated house, never deciding on a final number of rooms or the height of the ceilings. On rainy days, we'd make plans to go walking in the countryside that would dissolve the second we brought up their possibility. We'd be prudent with our money, and our daily thefts from the neighborhood supermarket would fill us with a sense of omnipotence. In the evening, I would carefully sort out the bills and staple together credit card receipts while you dozed off in front of the predictable images of a news report on TV. Your clothes would litter the floors of the apartment, creating a mosaic of colors and fabrics that I'd take a picture of to flatter your artistic sensibilities. When I found myself on the verge of a nervous breakdown, depressed by some unfulfilled ambition, I'd find consolation by congratulating myself on having avoided cancer, addiction, and fatal car accidents. The bleak succession of weeks wouldn't wear us down and would even help consolidate our relationship, founded on our deliberately empty and ascetic lifestyle. We'd remove salt from our diets, we'd limit our usage of hot water during our weekly ablutions, and we'd maintain a strict compatibility in our sexual relations. Due to the purported toxicity of cleaning products, we'd neglect cleaning the house and let the dishes pile up in the sink. On the evenings when your exhaustion extended to its outermost limits, longer and sadder than a deserted runway, you'd move your lips without making a sound, and my only response would be an understanding smile. You'd begin to automatically turn your back to me in bed, and I'd soon forget the shape of your stomach, breasts, and genitals. I would obsessively guard the memory of when your hands first strayed to my inner thighs at the beginning of our relationship. We would never travel, for both economic reasons and fear of terrorist attacks in an increasingly dangerous world, and we'd sleep on an uncomfortable mattress set on the floor of a cheap apartment. The temperature in our bedroom would never rise above sixteen degrees and the window would provide only a small slit of light. Once a week, you'd force yourself to drink a bottle of white wine to give you the courage to endure my groping, but you'd still forbid me from kissing you on the mouth. Although you would continue taking the pill, you'd force me to use a condom. Our embraces would be appalling, carried out in an uncomfortable silence while all around us the screams and stomps of unmonitored children echoed throughout the paper-thin walls of our building. The only child we'd manage to conceive would refuse to leave your stomach and would wait until it reached the age of retirement to come out and take us to court for mistreatment. To avoid having to face his accusations and the cost of a lawyer, we'd be forced to abandon him in a shoebox in the back lot of a convenience store, taking care not to leave behind fingerprints or any other condemning evidence. You wouldn't make a big deal out of my heart problems, and you'd grind your teeth in your sleep. The bills would pile up in our letterbox, and we'd mutually consent to shut off the electricity Monday through Thursday. Our bodies would stiffen at the sound of the telephone, as if its ringing were a portent of impending disaster. After calmly debating the issue, we'd agree not to divorce, fearing that our respective grandmothers would stop depositing monthly checks into our bank accounts if we did. Any attempt at tenderness between us would be treated as a crime, and we'd be on alert for signs of malicious impulses in each other. Beginning at six in the evening, we'd avoid exchanging even the smallest trace of a smile, and every Sunday, in front of our plates of leeks and carrots, we'd promise to stay faithful to each other until death sweeps us away. I'd keep a list of your fears in a secret notebook, always ready to resort to this fatal weapon should you decide to leave me. I would remain constantly on guard while you fell into a state of complete apathy. You'd criticize me for the nostalgic thoughts I'd have the weakness to bring up during my moments of despair, and I'd blame your unhappiness for your unconvincing displays of indifference. The TV would be our only source of outside information, and our relationship with the world would be defined by bitterness. We'd carry out the most insignificant task with great solemnity, as if its success depended solely on the amount of repulsion we felt upon its completion. We'd have a strong sense of duty and mouths full of banal, everyday expressions. We'd take diet pills and measure the change in our weight every two hours. We'd spend weeks drafting letters of complaint to the owners of our building, which would end up covered in mold behind our apartment's radiators. We'd never feel at peace and every day would be an anxiety-ridden wait for a crisis that would never occur. When our thoughts calmed down with the arrival of evening, we would force ourselves to stay up the entire night for the sole purpose of testing our resistance to fatigue. I'd become cowardly and frugal, monitoring our smallest expenses and discreetly sliding my fingers into soda machines in the hopes of gaining a few extra cents. I'd feel guilty when the shadow of a regret passed through my brain and, eventually, I'd decompose tormented by the memory of the years I lived before I knew you.

You're attracted to me, my presence comforts you, yet all my attempts at seducing you fall flat. I can decipher the minute details in your facial expressions, and I see the aircraft in your imagination burst into flames when I speak to you. You're incapable of resisting my charm or sarcastic outbursts of humor, which I sprinkle in careful doses over our interactions, and the compliments I repeatedly give you make swift and devastating raids into your childlike soul. I can be intolerably uptight, but you've yet to notice. So as not to frighten you and to increase my chances of continuing to see you, I keep my emotions in check, hiding my pain in the most unreachable depths of my heart. The blunt story of my first suicide attempt at thirteen made you laugh until you cried, and I use a subtle energy to provide you with the feeling of lightness lacking in your existence. You find my face intriguing and experience a vague curiosity at the thought that we could make love to each other. In certain looks you throw me in the cafeteria, I sense the dark instinct that prevents you from pushing our adventure any further. You are my catastrophe, my ideal, the one great opportunity life has offered me. You exist outside of time and beyond the reach of deterioration. You're so beautiful that my eyes grow exhausted looking for you in a crowd. In an excess of platonic perfection, I've had to put a cross on my libido to fool you about the supposed reasons I've chosen to be abstinent. May God prevent me from ever touching you, taking in your scent, or tasting your tongue. May a swift, cruel death put an end to the senseless attraction I feel toward you.

Reservation

SHE'S MANAGED TO stay thin, she must be sixty or sixty-two years old. She's placed her cardigan on the back of her chair and stands in the center of the room. Her skin glistens with sweat, and she pays close attention to every sensation that passes through her body. She turns her back to the window. She seems somewhat bored, or perhaps she's simply realized that since she's entered the room, her movements no longer feel entirely natural or innocent. As soon as the door was closed behind her, she placed her purse on the nightstand and took off her shoes. It's a simple room, containing nothing unusual. The carpet is a gaudy, acidic shade of green. The walls are colorless. A black and white photo of an alpine countryside hangs above the bed. She'll make no effort to appropriate this space or to familiarize herself with the objects that surround her. Even exhausted, she hasn't lost her aura of self-control. She lives less than one hundred kilometers from here in a simple but comfortable house with a veranda, on which she likes to stretch out at the beginning of the afternoon when the sun is at its brightest. She has very charming and caring friends who have courted her for years and whose advances she consistently turns down without taking the time to consider their merits or imagine their shortcomings, a habit that first developed out of an overpowering conviction that she should live her whole life a woman dedicated to only one true love, whether he be missing or dead, and which later became engrained from her years of living alone. Her face is never altered by sadness, and petty annoyances sometimes make her act like a stubborn and temperamental young girl. She pays no attention to the appalling houses that have sprung up like mushrooms near her house and disfigured the surrounding countryside. She isn't shocked by the violent images shown on TV and has never considered subscribing to either optimism or its opposite to make sense of what she sees. Her entire life she's sought out a state of mind where everything will be bright and make sense. She's here, in her sky-blue evening gown, dressed as if she had a date and was expected somewhere, perhaps on a café terrace or in the dim light of a classy restaurant. The room is filled with that particular silence one usually finds in hotels, an artificial, manufactured silence that keeps out the noises of the street. Last year, she walked through the avenues of New York without feeling overwhelmed or out of place. She was a champion of long distance running when she was fourteen and placed first in a regional competition. During the same period of her life, she discovered that she had exceptional talents for singing and dancing, neither of which she took the time to develop. At nineteen, she forced herself to lose weight after having been told her entire childhood that she was fat. At twenty, she posed nude for an aspiring painter who never became famous. She loves the look of used books and of streets at sunset. She would love to live without regret and to be able to spend money without hesitation. She's slept alone in her bed for as long as she can remember and has almost no memories from the chaotic and complicated relationships she maintained during her youth. Like the numerous setbacks she's been through, which have little by little weakened her morale and hollowed out her ambitions, her frustrations exist outside herself, in a region peripheral to her consciousness on some tiny beach, precariously sheltered from the wind and the waves. She turns toward the window. Outside, a calm but eager upper-class crowd has gathered in front of the steps of a theatre. The people are too far away for her to make out their faces, but she can sense the bottled-up excitement and dignified impatience of these men and women who in several minutes will be settling their backsides into the red velvet seats. She's never sought out harmony. She's come out of intense, short-lived relationships without feeling heartache, and she's never allowed herself to be worked into a rage. She's never tried to win somebody's respect, and she's walked away every time she's felt betrayed or misunderstood. She's often found refuge in rented houses. She has passionately loved snow, lakes, hills in the light of the setting sun, and the rusted hulls of boats in dry dock. She's spent a lot of time watching the movements of leaves and has nourished an endless curiosity for visual and tactile details while never taking the time to learn the names of the things that surround her. Her knowledge of science is limited and uneven, she's never felt an impulse to explore faraway places. She's always been slightly depressive and has always been aware of the destructive power that dwells within her like a nuclear weapon she's never had to resort to. She's happily avoided the anxious wait for a doctor's diagnosis and has known the sensation of having her life in immediate danger. She booked the room two weeks ago under a false name and took a photo of a blossoming cherry tree later that same day. She doesn't feel nervous, she's had all the time in the world to reflect on what she'd been doing with her life before she came here. Without trying to hide from the outside world, she slowly removes her dress with a practiced nonchalance. Since she stepped down from the train, she's felt as if her smallest actions have taken on a heavy significance, which she's decided to respect by pushing any skeptical thoughts out of her mind. During her first several hours in town, she wandered aimlessly under the April heat like a woman late for a date and desperate to be desired. Afraid that she might run into an old acquaintance to whom she'd have to give some kind of explanation, she kept her eyes on the ground and gave only a wavering attention to the other pedestrians, though she still raised her head to read the names of doctors and lawyers en-

graved into the gilded plaques attached to the town's buildings.
She paused in front of the art museum's closed doors. She drank
a coffee on a café terrace and exaggeratedly thanked the waiter
who brought her a glass of water. She sat down on a bench in a
small circular park. She imagined possible defense systems
against a variety of potential attacks. The Third World War
played out in her mind, she was forced to find a way to survive
in a deserted village where the buildings had been burnt down
and the inhabitants had been massacred by roaming hoards of
starving looters. In the sky, the blue became less intense. She
removed the watch from her wrist and wrapped it in a handkerchief. Upon entering the hotel lobby, her smile grew until the
space around her disappeared. The bathroom smells like soap.
She undresses completely and contemplates her breasts in the
mirror, then lets her eyes run over the rest of her body. She takes
a quick shower before putting on satin pajamas, beige with blue
glints. She continues to behave as if she were being watched. She
would like no other woman to be in her place, in this hotel
room, thinking thoughts other than her own. She won't die from
disease, and she won't suffer cognitive decline. She's never tried
to convert anyone's beliefs and has never felt sorry for herself.
She's read Epictetus and Conrad. She tells herself that she has
difficulties with concentration. It's always been easier for her to
focus her attention on the changing shape of a cloud than to
follow the progression of a sustained conversation. Useless attempts at making herself understood and accepted by those close
to her have ended in humiliation. Her coquetry, along with the
misunderstandings that have resulted from it, has gradually been
replaced by a superficial attitude of unfounded enthusiasm. She's
saved unopened letters in a shoebox. She's never been affectionate and has never fully divulged herself to anyone. The only arguments she's ever sought out are those proving that what she's
living through has a unique and profound meaning. She's often
made discoveries that could have irreversibly changed the course

of her life without ever making an effort to take advantage of them. She tells herself that because of secrecy and excessively convoluted sentences, she's become a stranger to her two daughters. The streetlights outside of the theater have been turned on, the setting sun throws a golden light on the facades of buildings and the edges of the sidewalk. She lies down and takes out a bottle of pills from her purse. Her thighs are pressed tightly together. She'll leave no explanation and will never learn the name of the play being performed across the street.

Off-Season

SHE WAS BORN on July 23; she stands one meter and seventy-four centimeters tall. Her identity card has been expired for two years now, and from all the available evidence, she has cut herself off from all past relationships. She's an athletic-looking blond, and she's living on the third floor of a small unattractive house, located less than a kilometer from the ocean. She's in good health, she moves quickly with an animalistic energy. She leads a sedentary existence and prepares herself daily to respond to the questions of a nonexistent judge who accuses her of having killed a banker for his refusal to give her a loan. As soon as night falls, she covers her bedroom's skylight and falls asleep several minutes later. She's inactive and regularly dreams of peaceful wildcats and yurts arranged in a half-circle on the slope of a snow-covered hill whisked over by wind. She subsists solely on cereal and canned food and consumes large amounts of instant coffee. She limits her electricity usage to the necessary minimum and brushes her teeth at least three times a day. She takes care of her body and strives to maintain a human appearance. She washes her clothes in a shower tray with soap from Marseille and always sleeps naked with one foot hanging out of her comforter. She's never felt sorry for herself and doesn't worry about how much longer she'll stay in the house. She never finds herself thinking deeply about her future or past, and she doesn't give in to the unexpected fantasies that infiltrate her imagination during moments of absentmindedness. Her first several days here, she left every morning to read the local newspaper near the

seaside, always in the same spot, but then began to space apart
her outings, slowly building up a system of natural defenses, as
thick as the walls of a fortified city, around her isolation. She's
never confided herself in anybody and has always had an acute
awareness of her solitude. She has no self-esteem but strikes
without hesitation whenever she feels threatened. She's im-
pressed her lovers with the violence of her orgasms, and her
perpetual silence has aroused incomprehension, even mistrust,
in others. As a child, she planned to leave humanity behind,
ready to renounce her mass of flesh to experience another version
of life on a gaseous planet where she would come into contact
with undiscovered beings. During a doctor's visit in middle
school, a school nurse pretended not to notice the cigarette
burns on her arms. She lacks warmth, her hands have never been
instruments of affection or tenderness. She broke into the house
where she's currently staying. It's surrounded on three sides by a
hedge of thujas and on the fourth by a white plastic fence. The
slate roof seems to be in good condition, and the red of its bricks
leaks over onto the white plaster façade, staining it the color of
blood. A cow and a pony graze in a neighboring field. Sometimes a tractor's motor breaks the ambient silence. She arrived
around three o'clock on a cloudy Monday afternoon, the sky was
gray, and she inspected the property in the day's dim light: a
living room, a kitchen, two upstairs bedrooms separated by a
bathroom. Later, when she'd turned the electricity back on, she
took in the house's details with indifference: the peeling wallpaper, the empty wardrobes filled with clothes hangers, the
grease-covered kitchen, the flower-patterned tablecloth on the
heavy oak table. Then she took an inventory of the objects left
behind in the drawers: a broken TV remote, dead batteries, brass
doorknobs, rubber washers, a miniature Swiss flag, an almanac
for the tides several years out of date. She reached the region by
hitchhiking, after having gone seventy kilometers by bus in the
company of small, talkative old women, wearing matching beige

raincoats, and several quiet teenagers keeping themselves occupied with chewing gum. With her eyes half-closed as she watched the countryside through the curtain of her eyelashes, she felt a sensation of extreme, even painful, slowness. Despite her sordid appearance, she didn't have to wait more than five minutes with her thumb up on the side of the road. First, there was a divorced mother, accompanied by her two daughters in a speeding Fiat, who took her about ten kilometers before dropping her off in front of a notary's office, then an unfriendly priest at the wheel of a white R5. Later, she had to ask the driver of a beige Citroen to stop in the middle of the countryside to avoid the complex story of his wife, who'd been undergoing chemotherapy for three years in a nearby hospital. She continued on foot, without a precise destination. She eventually saw, around a curve in the road, the sparkling of the sea above a field of colza. She later came across a squat chapel sitting on a bluff. She ate oysters and drank a bottle of white wine in a deserted restaurant overlooking the water. She visited a cannery and browsed through the brochures and maps in a tourist office watched over by a young woman in a wheelchair. She stole underwear from a supermarket and read the names on the graves of a small cemetery attached to a church whose roof was so low it seemed to almost touch the ground. She witnessed a conversation between a mother and daughter at a bus stop. The mother was scolding the daughter for her vulgarity. She must have been ninety-seven years old, her daughter seventy-eight. She had to consult a dentist in the nearest city for a toothache, she paid in cash claiming to have lost her papers. She slapped a teenager with a shaved nape who whistled at her in the street. She was approached by a stray dog with a hoarse bark. She vomited into a ditch. She read day-old newspapers and television guides abandoned on benches and stone walls. She saw old, fading advertisements on the facades of houses for sale. She bent down to inspect a detached, chubby arm from a plastic doll. She found a brand-new pair of sneakers, in her size, near the entrance of a city hall. She watched a funeral procession from a café terrace. On her way out of a dreary village, which looked like it'd come straight out of a movie set, she tripped on a rock and scratched her knee. At the entrance of another village, she saw a small old woman with crooked legs and a face suggesting insanity. She walked under the sun, through the rain and through storms, she sheltered herself beneath the roof of a shed, surrounded by the smell of oil, steel, and overripe apples. She stopped suddenly at her reflection in a window, surprised by the face of an ageless, sunburnt woman, whose green eyes seemed to send out warnings of distress or madness. She heard the distant notes of a bagpipe. She dried her face on a towel hanging from a laundry line. On a small bridge, her steps echoed hollowly. At times her thirst grew so severe that she considered breaking into the first house she saw and helping herself to a glass of water from the kitchen sink while the dumbfounded faces of a family eating dinner silently watched her. She began leaving the house less and less often to avoid being identified, preferring to go out only at the end of the day wearing sunglasses and a handkerchief tied around her head to make herself look older. She made an inspection of the house's exterior, then forced open the door of a picture window with the help of a steel sheet she found at the back of the garden. The living room furniture is outdated and mismatched, like what one would expect to find in a rental house. The dishes are all of different colors, and the curtains, carpets, and couch covers are impregnated with the stench of cold tobacco. Her library consists of approximately ten books piled in a gothic niche built into a living room wall: a novel by Bazin, moisture-swollen tourist guides missing pages that have been deliberately torn out, a collection of heavily illustrated books on deportation, and a pamphlet of Latin law terms. She reads and rereads the postcards inserted into the books, having difficulty believing in the existence of either the sender or the receiver. They could have been written by a melancholic chimpanzee describing his stay at a sanatorium to an encaged female partner. They might disclose, in a powerfully suggestive language, the mystic love of a provincial veterinarian for his disabled niece. She is already forty-three years old. She intensely studied judo during her years at university. She maintained an exotic and long-lasting relationship, devoid of any poetics, with a schizophrenic student who refused, even during sex, to remove his earphones, usually not bothering to take off his socks or warped T-shirts either. She no longer remembers whether he was Bulgarian or Romanian, and she could never pronounce his name correctly. She can't recall him asking a single question about her life or ever suggesting that they leave the university dorm room in which they lived reclusively for nearly three years, nourishing themselves exclusively on soda and pizza. She's never been inspired by human relationships and has never felt connected to her gender by anything more than a tautly pulled string, ready to snap with the slightest plucking. She's always known that she's unreachable on her plane of existence, and she often feels as if she's misplaced her body somewhere, like an umbrella forgotten on a seat in a café. Few things excite her. She doesn't know what it's like to daydream, but she's never been able to use her imagination to project herself into the future. She gets nauseous at the sight of a hair on the edge of a mustard jar and would be willing to kill anybody who tried to eat from her plate. She isn't sensitive to body odor and is unimpressed by people who can express themselves gracefully, using turns of phrase she's unfamiliar with. She's endowed with an average level of intelligence and is uncomfortable with abstraction. She's always been satisfied with simple and irrefutable bits of information, which allow her to move through a world whose subtleties are often lost on her. She takes long walks on a coastal trail marked with white and red lines painted on rocks and posts, and often runs into elderly couples, sometimes foreign, dressed in the same unstylish fashion. She passes by signs, their arrows turned toward the ground, which indicate megaliths, an equestrian center, or a chapel built in the thirteenth century. She considers with detached attention the sand-covered blockhouses, ruins of concrete stranded on the beach. She tries vainly to conjure up scenes of some former battle. The heads of surfers waiting for a wave appear on the ocean, which from a distance look like the heads of dogs rising up out of the water. Both night and day she listens to the mute rumble of the ocean, the crashing of the waves that come to die on the pebbles of the beach. The telephone once rang several times in a row on the same day. Then never again. In the days that followed, she could hear the noises of a prowler outside the house. More than a week went by before she heard a key in the front door, followed by the sound of a man's footsteps on the living room tiles and then the stairs. After sinking into the bathtub and grinding her cigarette out in an ashtray, she became motionless. The man who soon appeared in the doorway seemed somehow familiar. He had a thin mustache and was wearing a pair of faded jeans and a plaid shirt with the sleeves rolled up. He was either a fisherman or a mason, a farmer or a truck driver. He was handsome and, although he was larger and more rugged, looked slightly like her brother. He was younger than her, and she could picture his muscular back. He visited abandoned houses in the hope of finding a kidnapped princess tied to a torture rack. He suffered from a debilitating shyness and would remain single until the end of his life, paralyzed by fear every time he felt attracted toward a woman. If she hadn't been there, he would have spent a long time staring at himself in the mirror, striking lewd poses and trying on a g-string and bra found in the closet. The portable radio transmitted a muffled broadcast from a nightstand in the neighboring bedroom. Voices, which sounded as if they were struggling against the static, strained to reach them in the bathroom. She might have felt vulnerable and screamed at him to leave. She might have stood up and gotten dressed, modestly crossing her arms over her breasts and asking him to hand her the robe hanging on the door. She might have casually invited him to share a can of raviolis with her in the living room. She would have put him at ease, addressing him like a lover as she dried her hair. She would have insisted that he come with her into the bedroom to help her find a dress. The moment she saw the first signs of desire, she would have placed her hand on his arm with a furtive touch, somewhat out of place and unintentionally deterrent, and asked him to go back downstairs. She would have kept her eyes on him and avoided turning her back, fearing that he might try to flee. She would have treated him like a hesitant lover, making repeated references to her loneliness while assuring herself through indirect questioning that he was free of any venereal diseases. He would have found confidence in himself as he tried to paint his monotonous life in a favorable light. He would have stumbled during his attempts to explain why, at the age of thirty, he was still living with his mother. When she finally had the feeling of having triumphed over him, she would lead him to a nightclub not far from the house. They would sway together on the empty dance floor, and he would become increasingly sensual. She would feel his heavy breathing on her face and would laugh with her head thrown back. When he at last seemed drunk, she would pull him firmly toward her body and place her lips over his. She would ask him to accompany her to the bathroom, taking him by the hand like a fitful little boy. But, instead, she chose to stay silent and wait for his reaction. She noticed a movement of repulsion when their eyes first met. Maybe he was frightened by her long wet hair, which stuck to her shoulders like dead algae. Maybe she reminded him of a drowned woman in a horror film, or perhaps he thought she was planning to cut him into pieces after fertilizing herself with his seed. He mumbled something that sounded like an apology and then closed the door silently behind him. It's seven in the evening, and she's alone again. She listens to the roar of the waves breaking on the pebbles. She's ready to move on.

Delay

SHE PASSES THROUGH the dense crowd in the train station, she carries no luggage, and she doesn't notice the faces that turn to look at her. The metallic beams built into the station's glass façade project hard shadows onto the floor, outside the light is white, and the taxis honk as if it were the beginning of an uprising. To her right, a teenager sits drumming nervously on his guitar case as a redheaded girl comes up and squats down beside him, blowing bubbles with her gum that she collapses loudly, as if trying to get some reaction out of him. She hears the cries of children, the weakened, anguished voice of a mother. It's the month of July, a day of important departures and long waits at tollbooths and airports. This morning, she ate tuna rillettes spread onto toast and spent a long time studying herself in the kitchen sink mirror while repeating her age. Undifferentiated travelers, whose eyes she avoids like a deadly pandemic, brush up against her. She's been jobless for eighteen months now, and she harbors the remnants of a poorly cared for bronchitis. Earlier, she walked aimlessly through the streets and drank several cups of coffee in a deserted cafeteria. Her heels are too high, and her low-cut red dress gives her the feeling of having been invited to a ceremony whose purpose she's forgotten. She feels as if exhaustion, like some perception-altering virus, has taken root in the cells and marrow of her body. She'd like to be lying in a large, comfortable bed with clean sheets someplace far away from here, in a hotel room with soundproofed windows. She would unplug the telephone and refuse to open the door for the cleaning woman. She would let the sink run cold water to freshen up the room and to hydrate her drought-stricken mind. Her days would drag by with an excruciating slowness, but, as if it was normal to spend every minute in a state of suffering, she would never consider alternative ways of passing her time. She'd forget to eat and refuse to step out of bed, replaying in her imagination the details of a body that she would invent for the sole purpose of experiencing the pain of its absence. She would give herself fleeting and unsatisfying orgasms made up of small, rapid contractions, her body curled up in a position more reminiscent of pain than of pleasure. She would be completely out of reach, erecting a silent resistance to the exterior world, and the city surrounding her, weary from all its failed attempts to lure her back, would end up fleeing her forever: the city, with its streets, its buildings, its roofs and buses and inhabitants, would reestablish itself thousands of kilometers away from her in the middle of the desert. After she'd left the cafeteria, the Muzak continued to echo in her head like a sharp, syrupy jingle. She stopped to address a woman who, although she was at least twenty years older, strangely resembled her. She had the same black hair, the same nose, and, what she thought of as her best feature, the same supple legs. So that she might know her state of mind in twenty years time, she watched the woman with a studious intensity. After several seconds of silence, she asked for directions to the women's hospital but changed her mind when the woman offered to accompany her there. Two streets later, she began to feel lonely and longed for the company of someone who could understand her without first having to know her, someone who could take total control over their decisions while she gave willingly into the euphoric drunkenness of living each moment to its fullest potential. As evening set in, she became exhausted from her day of walking, and her ears started buzzing as if her brain was trying to rewire the severed connections of a thousand neural pathways. To avoid returning home, she took refuge in a car parked in front of her building. The car's interior smelled like cold ash, and the seat covers were worn out and streaked with grease. After thoroughly searching the car's contents in an attempt to better appropriate her new living space, she was able to sketch a rough mental portrait of its owner. With one hand placed on the steering wheel, she played with the radio dials in the darkness. Then, hoping for sleep, she reclined her seat and closed her eyes. In the morning, a sort of giant bent over to look at her through the passenger-side window before opening the door and saying, as he lowered himself into the seat, Hello, baby, how about driving me to paradise? Although his face was disfigured by pockmarks, it was his voice that disgusted her most. She let him run his hand over her breasts, promising she wouldn't tell the police. When he'd finished with her, the man thanked her politely, left the vehicle to squeeze himself into a car parked across the street, and then squealed away. Without checking its destination, she climbs onto the first train that arrives. As soon as she's settled into a window seat, she closes her eyes and falls fast asleep, cradled by the rhythm of the train's movement. She senses the smooth progression of buildings along the tracks, she visualizes deserted playgrounds enclosed by deteriorating fences. She has no plans for the future; for several days now, she's made no effort to distract herself by searching through her vault of memories. She shows no signs of life, and she's willing to sleep under bridges if she has to, preferring the painless company of herself to the invasive presence of others. She listens to the arrhythmic beating of her heart, from which seem to ooze applause and laughter, as if it was a small red theater overcrowded with restless homunculi trying to push their way to the exit. Alerted by a suspicious odor seeping out from under the cracks of her apartment, her neighbors, who have treated her coldly since the day she turned down their dinner invitation, will take it upon themselves to notify the police of her absence. They'll give up the idea of organizing a search party after having combed her apartment high and low without finding a single hint of who she was. The proprietors will deny ever having met her, claiming that the apartment has been vacant since a student of political economy killed herself in it after having repeatedly harassed them with phone calls in which she claimed to be their daughter, who had drowned at a summer camp twenty years earlier. Her appearance on Earth will be written off as a paranormal phenomenon, the result of a nervous influx in the brain of a one-eyed dog crossing a country road. Her belongings will be given away to charity, and the blue leather vest she received on her eighteenth birthday will be worn by a divorced woman working as a bartender. Two years later, the building and its surroundings will be torn down so that the neighborhood can be rebuilt with spacious apartment buildings, tree-shaded terraces, and high-end fashion boutiques kept well-stocked by helicopters arriving at all hours of the day. They'll find a way to make the sea levels rise and construct an artificial island that will hold the annual international festival of pornographic films. Her name will appear in the credits of a short film that will be completely ignored by critics. A man in a sky-blue suit, sweating and breathing with difficulty, wakes her up by sitting down heavily beside her. Outside, fields saturated with nitrogen and pesticides offer up their black surface to the sun's rays, the tarp of a briefly seen truck reminds her that a road runs parallel to the train tracks.

"I've been looking for you everywhere, what are you doing here?"

"I'm sorry, sir, I don't think I know you."

"You're tired, we should get off at the next station."'

"Please, leave me alone."

She closes her eyes to signal her unavailability to her neighbor. He goes on speaking in a pleading voice, made hoarse by tears and lack of sleep. The scent of deodorant mixed with the sour odor of sweat sends out bits of information that, like a data-starved computer, she can't help but analyze. She senses his cowardice and idiotic attachment to family values, and she imagines the suffocating straitjacket in which he imprisons his thoughts, fearing that they might upset the orderly and well-oiled rotation of his daily routine. He's of average intelligence and has little talent for abstraction. He imposes upon himself a strict regimen of mental exercises meant to slow the effects of premature cognitive decline and willingly agrees to work overtime in hopes of obtaining a promotion. He's excessively modest and, after ten years of marriage, still uses his hand to cover his penis when his wife unexpectedly comes into the bathroom. He experiences an unhealthy urge to talk about his phobias and he invents shortcomings for the sole purpose and pleasure of confessing them to her. He's haunted by traumatizing childhood memories of monotonous Sundays spent in an isolated vacation home that was frequented by transients. He proceeded methodically while courting his wife, employing the sales techniques he'd learned while studying for his business degree. He tried to make love to her on their honeymoon but, despite long and humiliating efforts, failed, and from that moment on their relationship, as if made out clay, began to gradually crumble apart. He'll go on loving her naively and sincerely until the end of his life, still talking to his only remaining photo of her, a blurry picture taken in photo booth when they were fifteen years old and intoxicated, during his last seconds on Earth. The man stands up, disappointed with her reaction to his presence, and walks toward the toilets, almost tripping in the aisle. From behind, he reminds her of an old widower she once came across crying in a park. His face was shiny and pink, the tears dripped down his face like a desire for oblivion. For the first and only time in her life, for no discernible reason, she wished that she were pregnant. When, out of either compassion or curiosity, she proposed that he come home with her to her apartment, he became immediately upset and began treating her as if she were a whore. A ticket checker wakes her up by shaking her shoulder, asks where she's going. She hands him her ID in response. The man says: Your name is Mona, you live at 6 Noire Street in a filthy and depressing apartment that you are afraid to leave for fear that you might be kicked out while you are gone, and as he fills out the fine in his notebook, she furtively looks over the fraying hem of his pants and the thin layer of dust on his shoes. She burned every photo she had of herself in the kitchen sink, along with her school notebooks and any document she could find containing her handwriting, and she wondered how many years it would take for all evidence of her existence to disappear from the face of the planet. She ripped down her bedroom's wallpaper and tore up the apartment's carpets, fearing that they might contain a stray hair that could be used to identify her. She sealed her memories in waterproof containers and sent them off on a cargo ship bound for nowhere. As if in preparation for embalmment, she carefully tweezed her body and took several consecutive baths. She spread out an assortment of dirty objects on her floor, which she'd collected in the previous days during her long walks, and after taking an inventory, she extrapolated from them the beginnings of a new existence, consisting of nothing more than these pieces of junk. She pictured her body being dismantled like a factory and then reconstructed from new, individual parts. From a pay phone near the entrance of her building, she reserved three different hotel rooms located at three distant locations for the same night. On the rare letters she received, she scribbled Unknown at this address, and she contacted a funeral home to obtain a burial quote that would ensure the utmost secrecy regarding the circumstances of her death, and the state of decomposition of her corpse at the time of cremation would be respected. She listened to the same song on repeat, never tiring of the strings' slow and somber lamento that was able to plunge her twenty-thousand leagues under the sea, on board a submarine with limited oxygen reserves. Every time she bought a sandwich from the neighborhood bakery, she had the face of a woman who had just been accused of some terrible crime. A woman sits down beside her, unfolding a newspaper in which she messily underlines the headlines in red ink. An unexpected braking sends the passengers' bodies jerkily forward. The train has stopped in the middle of nowhere. A crackling precedes an incomprehensible announcement muttered from the overhead speakers. Complaints can be heard throughout the train. She listens to the indistinguishable voices. Taking advantage of the confusion, her neighbor leans toward her and, as if sharing a secret, whispers: "I'm a clairvoyant; give me your hand." "I don't have any money to give you." "Don't talk, just listen." She fled an abusive father who would wake her up in the middle of the night and ask her to describe, scene by scene, her dreams in which she alternatively played the role of victim and executioner. She fled the dark forest in which she found herself every night, forced to count the number of trees to be felled while being chased by a choir of invisible chainsaws. She fled the oppression of a telephone that rang every Sunday at dawn like a memento mori. She fled the feeling she'd had, beginning during her difficult adolescence, of wearing rented outfits on which she left no trace of herself besides a scent of fear. At only five years old, she was fleeing eye contact like the plague, and later she would only allow herself to enter sexual relationships with partners who refused to take the time to kiss or caress her and who she was sure she'd never see again. She learned to read using a dictionary of mental illnesses, and her first drawings were of villages surrounded by high walls that she decorated with windblown banners. She fled the hateful and exhausting company of herself, which forced her each and every day to confront her inability to find satisfaction. She feels a warm numbness pass through her and the beginnings of a self-induced stomachache: a drill delicately pierces her skin and sinks into the depths of her being, twisting into her entrails until it finds an immaculately dark bedroom. The voice from the speaker asks for patience and gives an estimate of the stop's duration, which is immediately followed by more sighs and complaints. She believes none of it, preparing herself for the worst. The train is trapped, and the countdown has begun. A dangerous criminal, carrying a sample of a deadly and highly contagious virus created by a team of well-intentioned scientists in the depths of some laboratory, has boarded the train. The exits are sealed until further notice, a rumor that the passengers are condemned to die of hunger, asphyxiation, or blunt force trauma will spread quickly through the train, the most anxious passengers cutting their sufferings short by succumbing to heart attacks. Highly trained soldiers surround the train, instructed to kill without warning any passenger who tries to get off. The roads are barricaded, and access to any village within thirty kilometers is closed. She imagines: TV channels around the world broadcasting aerial images of the train. She hears: the public's opinions regarding the fate of the passengers and the potential risk of contamination if they are allowed to get off. Once all the passengers have died, orders will be given to proceed with the complete destruction of the train by missile. Through her window, she can see the cooling towers of a nuclear power plant rising up out of the cornfields. She suddenly remembers that she forgot to turn off a radio somewhere, unless a new tenant has taken possession of her brain, covering the walls with vengeful love letters written in lipstick. In the train, the conversations resume again after a moment of silence, grow animated, get louder. She predicts that panic will soon take hold of them all, causing some to ball up in fright and others to scream while banging their fists against the windows. She foresees: soldiers ambushing the train, the infrared scopes of their machine guns fixed on the train's exits, ready to fire at any suspicious movement. She stands up and moves toward the other end of the train. The door makes a hissing sound as it slides open. Time seems to drag by. A gust of hot air, filled with minute particles and the nauseating odor of oil and steel, rises up from the gravel. Paying no attention to the men and women who watch her from behind the safety of their windows, she walks along the tracks toward the front of the train. She's calm and focused. Night hasn't yet fallen, a red sunset reflects off the rails. Behind her, everything seems languid and unreal. She feels scornful and uncertain. She breathes steadily and goes on walking, her feet bare, along the iron tracks.

Infiltration

SHE WALKS INTO the concrete building under a thudding rain, holding a pale, feeble boy by the hand. They pass in front of the rows of letter boxes and step around a puddle of water as they enter the elevator. She stares at herself reluctantly in the elevator mirror: her freezing, wet hair frames her unexpressive face, highlighting the circles under her eyes and her excessively protruding cheekbones, both of which seem to reflect the sorrowful neglect she's shown herself over the years. The child beside her is wearing rubber boots and a yellow raincoat, his face is still and solemn. As if the entirety of his attention was focused on some mental exercise. The succession of gray doors and the water pipes running endlessly through the hallways make her envision a city of canals buried hundreds of meters beneath the ground. Their apartment is decorated in a simple, neutral fashion, without ostentation. After a number of taxing efforts, and after replacing the apartment's wallpaper, she's managed to create a precise and orderly environment, distinguished by an admirable cleanliness. The ageless pine cabinets house only the products necessary for their own cleaning, and the photos of landscapes lend the apartment an understated elegance. The smell of dampness, impossible to get rid of, isn't immediately noticeable. Last week, she carried the last moving boxes down to the building's dumpsters, feeling a slightly disturbing relief at the idea that she'd found an appropriate, even natural, place for every one of her possessions. She employed a simple pragmatism and didn't allow herself to become discouraged by the task, reminding herself to solve the problems one by one, working at a comfortable pace with a realistic belief in her abilities, and found herself afterward considering their future together. She could tell herself that a new life was beginning for her and her child, one allowing her to form new connections with the world and to search out certain experiences whose value she could now better understand, while taking a novel but guarded interest in things capable of moving her, surprising her, or frustrating her, things whose existence she had until then been unaware of. In the hope of leaving behind the confusion that had reigned over the years of her marriage, a time during which she was forced to live in the perpetual and demoralizing misery of a regulated and static existence, she planned to let herself dream, and this modest apartment situated on the seventeenth floor, ideal for helping her rediscover her sense of dignity, was the symbol of this new beginning. Upon returning from school, the child's routine is to remove his boots, wash his hands, and then go silently into his bedroom, each step completed automatically, as if he was acting under orders or his muscles had been taken over by invisible cogs. The child usually occupies himself with drawing or puzzles while she prepares the meals, which she announces to him with a forced cheerfulness. In his notebook, he draws five-legged dragons and mutilated figures whose bodies lack organic substance and are made up entirely of electric wires and metallic engines. He's meticulous and methodical and employs terms as precise as propeller blade, nervous system, and genital organs, and in every task he undertakes he uses an analytical deliberation that frightens her. At the age of two and a half, he could take apart and rebuild a fan with astonishing ease. On Sundays, they examine the skeletons on display at the natural history museum or take a walk through the park, hand in hand, matching the rhythm of the other walkers. He rarely speaks during these outings and, unable to ignore a sensation of being judged by him, she feels his half-worried, half-inquisitive stare permanently fixed on her. She's tired of his dullness and unchanging personality, and at times, the thought that she's all he has in the world overwhelms her. His new teacher, with whom she spoke on the first day of school, suggested making him take up a sport to put him into contact with other children. She sometimes sees him as a stranger who one day decided to enter her life when she'd forgotten to lock the door, and he seems to cease existing the moment he's outside of her field of vision. She can't remember ever having been pregnant, and it often requires conscious efforts to remind herself to think of him as a child, defined, like other children, by an intelligence and by limitations that correspond to his age. When she calls him by his name or shows him affection, his neck tightens and his face goes blank. She'd love to be a generous and energetic mother, surrounding her child with all sorts of unnecessary and tender displays of affection to assure him of her love. She would write naïve stories for him, inspired by her unwavering faith in the existence of moral values in a world where nothing happens without a reason, she would act like an older sister, protective but easygoing, capable of scolding him without ever coming off as unfair. She sometimes wishes she could make a harmless abstraction out of their bad beginnings, and she strives to erase any trace of their past from her memory. When she speaks to the child about his father, respecting a promise she made to herself to keep nothing hidden from him no matter what it might cost her, her voice takes on a metallic timbre to describe the insipid, incomplete, and inconsequential man, toward whom she still feels a lingering anger. It seems as if an eternity has gone by since they moved in, and the constant rain has drawn a thin, dark curtain between them and the world. She's cheerless and stagnant, and when she turns her back to the child, he watches her skinny, austere shadow silhouetted by the backlight from the window. Before her marriage, she saw a psychologist in a dark, antiquated office whose tiny gray eyes disappeared behind the reflection of his oversized glasses. She

worked as a proofreader in a publishing house and read dozens
of pornographic books filled with violence and sadism. She was
terrified of becoming mentally ill during this period of her life,
and hoping to conceal from others the invasive images that so
often filled her mind, she taught herself how to breakdown the
creations of her consciousness into meaningless grains of sand.
She can remember the exact color of her hair at that time, and
a little alarm clock with phosphorescent hands that watched
over her after nightfall. Not knowing why, she sits frozen in the
bathroom and watches the water run freely into the bathtub
while telling herself that inactivity is a greater torture than any
form of work. She doesn't speak much and her smile, when she
tries to appear friendly, is fleeting and joyless. She applied for a
job in a small hotel situated between a prosthetics store and a
run-down building, destined for demolition, at an intersection
on the city's ring road. During her interview, she responded to
the questions confidently and without hesitation, feeling as if
someone had taken over her voice with the intention of pushing
her toward the highest levels of success. She hadn't said a word
for days, and the ease with which she spoke was disturbing.
When she returned home, the front of her building looked so
dismal and so hostile in the twilight that she had difficulty believing that waiting for them, almost all the way at the top, was
their calm and tidy apartment, hot and damp and filled with
conventional furniture. The next evening, after her first shift at
work, she got off on the wrong floor and almost broke her key
in the lock of an unmarked door. She never crosses anyone in
the hallway, and the cars in the parking lot never seem to move
from their places. She sometimes feels as if she's the building's
only inhabitant, and when she walks through the streets on her
way to the hotel, a distance the size of the Sahara seems to sep-
arate her from the other pedestrians. On evenings when the rain
lets up, she thinks she can hear her son's heart beating in her
chest, and she experiences a feeling of uncontrollable and irra-

tional power. One morning, as she was filling a glass with water from the kitchen sink, she saw a ball of black hair floating in the liquid and almost threw up. Afraid of coming home late, she automatically declines invitations to dinner parties or the theater, and at lunch breaks, she prefers to isolate herself in a cafeteria for several minutes of recovery, letting her thoughts wander while her coffee gets cold. One day, she noticed a patch of moisture on the ceiling above her bed whose shape seems to change daily, and she still hasn't solved the mystery of whether or not it was there before they moved in. She tries not to stare at it, but several times a day, her attention gets diverted and, as if the moisture was infusing itself drop by drop into her thoughts, her eyes move immediately to the patch. One evening, she lingered in town as the stores began closing, strolling aimlessly through the streets in a state of euphoria, with the feeling that she was expected at some imprecise location. She went into a laundromat, seated herself in front of a noisy washing machine, then got up and left after realizing she had no reason to be there. She asked for directions from a woman who shared a slight resemblance with her, hoping she'd take an interest in her life, and later she offered to help an old man cross the street, who thanked her distrustfully when she proposed to come home with him to help with his errands and housekeeping. She felt radiant and carefree, and she made an appointment for the following day in a hair salon that she'd never set foot in again. She wandered through unknown streets that seemed to be an extension of her own flesh and being, with a sensation that by moving through, the city she was moving also through her own body, feeling free and confident in herself, almost like a true, desirable woman, up until the moment she saw the time in a jewelry store's display case. She was welcomed to the school with a cold smile from the principal, to whom she had to make up an excuse for being late, while the child, with an imperturbable and disquieting patience, went on drawing at the back of the class, seemingly unaware that she'd arrived. Her anxieties intensified. Every evening, as she opens the door to her apartment, she feels a disturbing hesitancy at the thought that her bedroom's ceiling has finally come crumbling down, causing water to rise several feet above the floor, the furniture pitching from one corner of the living room to the other while bills float on the surface. She dreams of waterlogged clothes, drowned bodies, and peeling wallpaper leftover in the rooms ravaged by the water's damage. Her days in the hotel lobby seem unending, absurdly hollow, almost intolerable. Some days, she fantasizes about falling gravely ill and staying bedridden for days, so that she could dedicate herself to following the hourly progression of the moisture patch, not missing a single moment of the spectacle. Lying in her bed, transformed mentally into a raft, with her eyes fixed on the ceiling, she'd have the feeling of flipping through the pages of a textbook on physiognomy or of searching for shapes in the clouds. She sometimes wakes up suddenly in the middle of the night and rushes into the bathroom, afraid that she'll find her son's drowned body floating in the bathtub. She focuses her ear toward the ceiling, her body motionless and tense. Her mental health is failing her, she can feel the pressure of pent up morbid thoughts, and she often comes home from the supermarket with products whose purpose she's forgotten, which she then hoards in the cupboards as if in preparation for a several-months-long siege. Facing the landlords' persistent silence and refusal to respond to her calls, she writes bitter, long-winded letters that she later finds folded and crumpled in the pockets of her rain jacket. For a second consecutive time, the pregnancy test is positive. She leans against the window and watches the cars permanently parked at the foot of the building, abandoned by their owners. It feels an eternity since she's been with a man, and in her desperation, she's considered putting a small announcement in the newspaper requesting the father to come forward. Having reseated herself behind the hotel counter, her hair done up, her

makeup carefully applied, she watches the hotel guests, trying
to guess which one of these men would agree to marry her and
lead a disciplined and honorable life at her side, a laudable existence free of shame or regret. The hours of waiting flow by
without any noticeable decline in her anxiety. Her fatigue in-
creases daily, and her recurring bouts of nausea have made her
progressively more irritable. In the evening, before passing by
the nursery to pick up the child, she makes a detour to the supermarket and buys a bottle of wine whose contents she'll empty
into the kitchen sink after failing to finish her first glass. She
catches a man in the lobby looking at her with a glimmer of
either kindness or empathy, and she feels as if her mind is suddenly at peace. As he hands her his room key, she sees in his
hesitant, almost shameful attitude a confession of uncertain attraction. His imprecise body is lost in his cheaply made clothes,
making him seem sad and empty, and the way he leans slightly
toward her hints at a concealed feebleness. Would he be willing
to propose to her? She sees herself naked, lying beside him. His
leg hairs are scattered, and his torso seems inflated, like a construction worker's or a stevedore's. Aside from these disappointing images, which seem to serve as a warning of their future
conjugal intimacy, she is powerless in imagining the circumstances of their first encounter. One morning, after he's left the
hotel at his usual time, she takes advantage of his absence to go
into his room. She searches through his drawers and jacket
pockets in search of evidence that would allow her to confidently establish that they share an irrefutable connection with each
other. She discovers a photo of his wife, a small, neat, insignificant blond posing in a freshly cut garden, flanked by two children with pink faces that shine with contentment, and she
thinks: his current life, so peaceful and mediocre, means nothing,
because in two months he'll have divorced her and lost all interest in his children, whom he'll view with perplexity and a sort
of cold detachment, as if they'd never been a part of his life.

Using soft words and delicate attention, she'll erect a psycholog-
ical barrier so dense between him and the rest of the world that
he'll no longer be able to live without her body, her caresses.
She'll become his obsession and his only reason to continue
living. A feverish desire will burn permanently in his eyes, she
tells herself while smelling his wrinkled clothing to better
immerse herself in their future, and he'll be unable to think of
anything but her. In her presence, he'll feel virile and accom-
plished, but a discouraging glance from her will suffice to throw
him into torments of doubt, sending him to his knees as he begs
her to forgive imaginary shortcomings and to never leave him.
He'll prove himself clumsy in handling his emotions and will
make repeated threats of suicide until the day she grows bored
with him and begins offering her body to strangers. She strokes
her breasts in front of the mirror, her vision blurred through
half-closed eyes, and then curls up in the bed as the scent of her
long, sprawling hair impregnates his pillow. He wasn't her type,
but that had little importance, because confident in her powers
of seduction, she would quickly have made him submit himself
to her entirely, erasing all the imperfections and defects that
tarnished his personality while rendering him attentive and
devoted, a flesh and blood reproduction of the man she'd always
dreamed of. They would make, she thinks with a half-smile of
contentment, a mismatched and pathetic couple, their life together obsessively regimented by the whim of her emotions
while he devotedly obeyed her smallest requests, and the damp
and modest apartment in the immense concrete tower would
dissolve into nothing more than a distant memory. On the day
of their wedding, her stomach would be large and round, and
he'd watch with a confrontational insecurity anyone appearing
to show suspicion over its paternity. The child would be next to
her, dressed in a suit with a white shirt and bowtie, looking like
a miniature, terrified, and serious adult. He wouldn't leave her
side for an instant, and she would on several occasions be obliged

to force him away. To make a diversion, people will compliment her on her dress and the exquisiteness of her bracelets. She will be carried dead drunk and unresponsive to a bedroom where the murmur of her reception will vibrate through the walls. When she wakes up, her stomach feels painful and swollen. Her eyes fixed on the ceiling, she recognizes the patch of moisture.

Quarantine

SHE STANDS IN the doorway of the house as the day's white light hits its facade, carving clean, sharp lines around her body. Her arms crossed, she watches the empty road stretch out into the distance. She seems imperturbable, her face is serious and contemplative and shows no sign of the anxieties that dwell in her mind, searching for a way to force a path into her consciousness. At more than an hour's walk from the nearest village, the house, its shutters closed, seems to have fallen into ruin. The lawn, scorched by the sun and the acid rains, has grown yellow. So that no one suspects she's there, she's let the flowers go without water and neglected the upkeep of the vegetable garden. The fruit trees haven't produced anything in an eternity. She isn't bothered by the heat, the extreme blondness of her hair isolates her from the rest of the world like an impassable wall. She experiences no feelings of melancholia, she knows which images she can summon to fight back the bouts of depression derived from her solitude. It's barely noon, but already the day seems close to extinction. She's given up listening to the news and now finds herself sitting in the living room's darkness on the rough linen couch. She takes a moment to look over the furniture and the rays of light falling over the wooden floorboards. She doesn't miss the city, and the memories of her past, made up of jobs, social ambitions, and aborted relationships, give her no sense of nostalgia. She doesn't regret her decision, and since she made it, her world has been reduced to the sensations readily available to her five senses. She doesn't care about calculating the precise

amount of time she's been here, it sometimes seems like she was
born to the house's walls and floors, growing up entirely alone
while living off of plaster dust, glue, and nails. Upon waking on
certain mornings, she finds herself dreading the day to come,
thinking that it will consist of a horrific and degrading slowness
that will cause her to suffer an imaginary torment far worse than
any real injury. Her body has become an exact reflection of her
soul. She coldly considers her hands and is reminded of the
fingernails of her mother, who at the height of her former splendor insisted that she possessed healing powers. She washes them
several times a day and, fearing an infection of the mouth, is sure
to always brush her teeth thoroughly. She's meticulous about
everything and rigorously monitors her personal hygiene, as if
following to the letter a military regimen, a doctor's prescription,
a divine order. She washes the floors, cleans the house, and
sponges the walls with a rabid energy: the smell of bleach infuses
her thoughts and clothing like an antiseptic obsession. She often
gets up in the middle of the night to check the state of the water
pipes or to make sure that her sweaters and blankets haven't been
devoured by mites. Sometimes she installs herself in the car
parked in the garage and falls deeply asleep, curled up in the
backseat after having inspected the contents of the glove com-
partment for the millionth time. Fearing that an intruder might
take it over or pillage her reserves of food during her absence,
she never strays far from the house. She's always on guard and
struggles against her natural inclination for comfort and tranquility. She can never relax or let her mind wander, even when
the house is securely locked. She goes into the kitchen and sinks
her teeth into potato peelings while watching her feet on the
tiles. She goes upstairs to check the bathrooms and inspect the
closets, always maintaining a maximum level of vigilance and
attentiveness. She carefully examines her surroundings, forcing
herself to breathe evenly in order to slow down her heart. She
slides her hands over the house's books, she's content to simply

read the titles written on their spines. She sometimes looks through a dictionary to exercise her memory and reassure herself that she's still capable of holding a coherent and logical conversation. With the help of numerous repeated readings, she's memorized by heart the definitions of pandemic, avian flu, virus, bacteria. She's learned how to master the whims of her imagination, and she can read the future in the flakes of paint peeling off the bathroom's walls. The telephone never rings, and she sometimes dials a number at random. One day, a hoarse voice answered, the voice of a woman who either hadn't slept or hadn't spoken for several days, a woman who was either deeply depressed or being held prisoner somewhere. She whispered rushed and frantic sentences, as if trying to hide her voice from the surveillance of someone in a neighboring room. She spoke of a dungeon in which everything was black and filthy, where she moped about helplessly while waiting to undergo a variety of abuses. She begged her to come and find her, to not let her spend another night there. Without a word of response, she hung up and unplugged the telephone. Wherever she goes, she carries her Swiss army knife and a portable radio with a built-in generator. When she can no longer stand hearing the pretense-filled government announcements hissing out toward her ears like stray bullets, she tunes the radio to one of the available foreign stations, whose monotone and incomprehensible output, punctured by cracks and static, soothingly reminds her of night-time drives from her childhood. When she's reminded of the fact that she possesses a body of her own, she can't resist the temptation of immersing herself in a boiling bath and putting on makeup as if in preparation for a night out, rebelling against her usual routine and the spirit of economy that normally drives her actions. She positions herself at her bedroom window and scrutinizes the universe outside as if she were looking through the lens of a microscope or from the lantern of a lighthouse in the middle of the ocean, isolated among the reefs more than ten thousand leagues from any continent. She began to keep a diary, but then, tired of searching for words and paralyzed by the idea that some stranger might find it after her death and take it upon themselves to publish it, gave up and began drafting the blueprints for an impenetrable fortress. In preparation for the possible intrusion, she sleeps upstairs with the window open to hear any suspicious noises. To help herself fall asleep, she mentally prepares her escape route several times in a row, removing the superfluous movements and parasitic thoughts that could slow her down. Her dreams carry her away to the heart of the taiga. One evening, as the day turns to twilight, she follows a paved road that leads to the postern of a deserted city overrun with wild vegetation. She advances with caution along the city's principal road, bordered on both sides by crumbling houses. She hesitantly enters one. It no longer has a door. A small tree grows in a corner. She meets the piercing eyes of a group of barn owls that immediately try to escape but collide first into the wall and then into her, entangling themselves in her clothes. Everywhere it's the same scene, the same desolation. She checks the expiration dates on boxes of old antibiotics while mentally preparing herself to face a wide range of trying scenarios. She strives to be uncompromising and tough, ready to confront any possible danger. She imagines that her hand is infected with tetanus, and she must carry out an immediate amputation. She imagines digging an underground tunnel for a secret evacuation in case of a siege. She imagines manufacturing handcrafted incendiary weapons from the reserves of rags and fuel. She cuts her hair and wears only pants, imposing upon herself a daily program of exercises while training for close-quarters combat with nonexistent enemies. She strains her eyes staring down the road through the droning heat, thinking she can make out long, burnt shadows in the air's vibrations, blown into exodus by a panicked wind. The planes that pass by in the sky are the only signs of humanity she's seen since she arrived here. She pictures the pilots in their cockpits, clean shaven and smelling of cologne. Should one of these machines take fire in midflight and come crashing down somewhere nearby, she would run immediately to the pilot, giving him the necessary treatment with the confidence and composure of an experienced nurse. She would drive him to the house and pamper him like a child during his convalescence, making sure, with the use of flattery and anxiolytics, that he never expressed a desire to go back to his old life. She would cut out revealing nightgowns from his parachute and fashion him djellabas that would give him the regality of an Arab prince. They would barricade themselves inside the house until they became nauseous at the sight of each other. After several weeks, they would no longer make any distinction between night and day and communicate exclusively with grunts and croaking. She would come to crave the taste of his sperm and cover him with her urine to mark him as her territory. He would die either of a heart attack, exhaustion, or boredom, and she would hastily bury him in the garden while recalling the funeral she and her younger brother gave a baby bird, fallen from its nest, when she was nine or ten years old. The next day, she would have forgotten his face and, as if their relationship had been a sick, grotesque episode in her life attributable only to the unpredictable impulses of her libido, take it upon herself to burn his clothing and destroy any trace of their intimacy. She's developed a habit of dissecting her problems and cutting into her uncertainties with the surgical precision of a coroner. She isn't poetic, she doesn't pity herself for what's happened in her life. She's never considered suicide. She doesn't glorify suffering, and she doesn't know what to do with her memories. She left, or, no, she was left by, a man who was either fair, cruel, or miserable, or some combination of the three. He beat her and showered her with gifts, and not a day went by that he didn't teach her a new method for contraception. His criticisms, his humiliations, his forced penetrations, she accepted everything about him with the practiced resignation of a saint or an alcoholic. One night, she heard a knock at the door. After waiting a moment hoping that the visitor would think the house was empty, she opened the door, armed with a wine bottle. She found a young woman, staring at her with curiosity: "I'm Alma." Her face was bruised and locks of sweaty hair covered her forehead. She was both younger and frailer, and she seemed to harbor a restless energy ready to explode at the slightest provocation. There was a trace of instability in her face, a diamond-like toughness, an uncultivated determination. Standing in the kitchen, she said she was a nurse and that she'd just been in a car accident. The man driving had died instantly. As she'd extricated herself from the car, she saw blood on his forehead and temples, and his hands were still wrapped tightly around the steering wheel. She'd wandered through the countryside, shouting for help and knocking on the doors of other houses without ever receiving a reply. She'd struggled through ditches and barbed wire. She'd lost one of her shoes without turning back to try and find it. She'd crossed through a forest and then continued straight at an intersection. She'd felt no fear, only a slight concern that someone might stop and ask her to justify her nocturnal presence on the road. After eating a microwaved hamburger steak accompanied by a small portion of peas, she agreed to sleep on the ground floor. She went to bed and stayed hidden away in her room the whole next day. Soon after her arrival, it began to rain relentlessly. The two women, having nothing to fill their time, stayed in the house and furtively watched one another. An epidemic could have been wreaking havoc throughout the rest of the world, sparking anarchy and decimating the global population with the speed of a galloping horse, while they went about their days in a protective bubble, isolated from the virus by the rain-drawn patterns on the windowpanes. Alma rarely spoke, the bruises faded from her face as if under the effect of a magic balm or some photographic technique designed to bring out the insolent youthfulness hiding in her features. She responded with reluctance to the most ordinary of questions, flatly refusing her companion's timid attempts at friendliness, who was trying by all means possible to come off as hospitable. Although there was no obvious resemblance between him and Alma, her brother, so young, so frail, so innocent, reappeared in her memory. All these years later, she found it fair and inevitable that he'd died at the age of nineteen from an acute leukemia, undergoing intensive treatments during the final weeks of his illness that served only to push him further and further away from life. While as for Alma, she was strong and obstinate, superficial and audacious. She never made compromises, and she compensated for a hearing disability by learning how to read lips. Her sentences were rough, cut up like boards fresh out of a sawmill. She would sometimes tell pointless, innocent lies, a habit no doubt carried over from her childhood, and she acted only in her own self-interest, never letting herself be softened by the hesitant attempts at affection that her beauty attracted. She was intractable, she could be brutally seductive, and her facial expressions seemed to annihilate the logic of arguments made in her presence. She was inconsiderate, and she immediately behaved as if she'd always lived in the house. Used to it from her days at boarding school, she wasn't surprised to have her bedsheets replaced on a regular basis, and she could spend unprecedented amounts of time sitting alone in a room doing nothing. She never took part in the preparation of meals, and she held her fork firmly in a fist. Wine didn't seem to make her drunk. One day, a stray dog tried to approach her: she threw a rock toward it and hit it in the eye, unable afterward to force back a smile of satisfaction. She showed signs of a formidable intelligence and couldn't stand seeing a household object go unused. She took apart and rebuilt electronics with a disturbing facility and locked herself away for an entire afternoon in the basement to repair a broken seat. On certain evenings, her bedroom light would stay on until the early morning. One

night, she could hear Alma opening and closing the red music
box on the chest of drawers near the foot of the stairs, then,
probably overcome with boredom, her footsteps began resonat-
ing through the house as she came up to the second floor. I can't
sleep, she said as she violently opened the bedroom door, a
wrinkle of malice digging into the center of her forehead. She
sat down on the edge of the bed without another word, and the
two women began a game of cards that went on into the middle
of the night. Sometimes they fell asleep cradled in each other's
arms. When the weather became nice again, Alma would put on
a swimsuit and spend the bulk of her day stretched out on a
chaise longue in the garden. Her skin turned brown, she seemed
to grow smaller. Her rare smiles seemed to be accidental, and she
judged it useless to utter a word of greeting when she came into
the kitchen each morning to pour herself a cup of coffee. She
took to walking barefoot and neglected to bathe for days at a
time. Her body began to give off the sickly sweet scent of river
water. Then one day, when the sky was gray, she announced her
desire to leave. It must have been the beginning of autumn, the
heat was less intense, and the countryside was beginning to fill
with red and yellow. After locking the doors of the house, they
took to the road, carrying a map, a compass, and some emergen-
cy rations. As soon as the house was out of sight, they felt light
and carefree, as if they'd escaped from a void, and the landscape
seemed to unfold before them like an invitation to boundless
possibilities. They walked briskly at each other's side without
exchanging a word, skirting around the neighboring villages
through overgrown trails and empty fields. From time to time,
they came across indifferent herds of animals that showed no
signs of noticing them. Isolated farms, whose outbuildings were
in ruin, seemed to welcome their arrival. Thinking she recognized their surroundings after two hours of walking, Alma
climbed onto a tractor to take a panoramic view of the horizon.
Sometime later, they found the gray Volvo overturned in a ditch.

The man's body had disappeared, and the traces of blood had been washed away by the rain. In the trunk they found a thermos, two flashlights, clothes, and a first aid kit. It was the middle of the afternoon. Fog was beginning to surround them, piling up in every direction as if hoping to block their passage. They returned to walking, convinced that sooner or later they would reach the coast.

Cohabitation

YOU'VE NEVER BEEN jealous, and you've shown an inexhaustible patience toward her. You welcomed her like a long-lost friend, rendered unrecognizable and repellant by the passage of years, whom you wanted to avoid making aware of everything that had separated you from one another. As understanding as always, and more careful than ever to preserve the harmony of our relationship, you never asked for any explanation regarding her continuous presence, and she quickly grew on us, becoming as indispensable to our happiness as the weather station we rely on for last-minute excuses to cancel our walks in the countryside or day trips to the sea. You've abstained from judging her, and you don't hold her mispronunciations of everyday words against her. You tolerate her lack of culture and her addiction to TV. You wish she'd be more sociable, or at least somewhat more affectionate, but your sympathy for her has proven to be unshakeable. Her complete lack of manners and unrelenting insolence upset you no more than the skimpy, insufficient outfits she wears out in the cold. Together, we've learned how to cope with the unpredictable caprice of her emotions, and the minor but irritating adjustments her arrival precipitated never put the stability of our relationship, built upon years of openness and sincerity, in peril. And that she was younger and even, according to some, more attractive than you never condemned her in your eyes.

I originally claimed to have seen her balled up like a fetus on the edge of the road, but confronted with the disbelief you showed this first version of events, I was forced to confess that I'd picked her up hitchhiking. In response to the precise questions you asked me, in a voice clearly altered by your fear of confirming certain unspoken suspicions, I deemed it best to respond imprecisely, fearing that I might contaminate your imagination with superfluous details. At no point did you have the pettiness to insinuate that she might be one of my patients, whom I'd numerous times in the past been weak enough to enter into fleeting affairs with, and for this, I was immeasurably grateful. You didn't cause a scene when I suggested that she stay the night, and the next day, you even offered to make her fried eggs for breakfast. The discreet tears you shed when we decided to keep her for an indefinite period of time didn't hurt my resolve at all in the matter, but I agreed to have a calm, explanatory conversation with you, something we hadn't needed to do in years. You're emotional and have a delicate constitution strongly resistant to change, but every time our relationship undergoes a crisis, you demonstrate a faultless loyalty and an admirable resignation, and in return for your understanding, I swear to never betray my promise to remain at your side until the end of my life. Faithful to the values learned during your privileged upbringing and keeping a close check on your impulses, you never stooped to anger or blackmail, and you made no objections when I proposed to integrate her more completely into the fabric of our life, like a newly purchased appliance whose qualities and advantages I'd repeatedly boasted about in front of you. You came out improved by this challenge, and my feelings toward you took on an unexpected mixture of respect and awe.

She entered our lives with such perfect submission that we could never find any reason to complain about her behavior. Aside from her disposition for sleeping in and her tendency to leave her clothes scattered throughout the house, she fit in so well to our way of life that we were soon able to overlook her foreign accent and her eccentricities. She was simpleminded, volatile, and unconcerned (at least from our perspective) with matters of hygiene. Although she wasn't, in the true sense of the word, helpful, she knew how to make herself useful and found a certain pleasure in tending the garden and taking care of the simple cleaning duties you had the presence of mind to assign her, evidence of the steady and unwavering trust you placed in her. We would have appreciated it if she'd read more and shown a more open and curious approach toward the world, but we still allowed her to use her free time as she pleased. As a display of our respect for her, we solicited her advice when buying a food processor and decorations for the house. She was exemplary in the presence of guests, and we had the foresight to avoid any of our friends who would have had the indiscretion to speak to her directly, embarrassing her with difficult and intrusive questions. After more than thirty years of living together, we were proud of our ability to welcome her into our home without disturbing the deeply ingrained order of our routines or chipping away at our strong attachment to certain long-standing habits favored in our household. She wasn't greedy, and she never thought to demand anything more from us than the reasonable sum of weekly pocket money we decided she deserved. The precepts we tried to instill in her, with her own benefit always in mind, caused no lasting damage to her personality. That we were never forced to scold her for misbehavior, due to her willingness to conform, is a point worth highlighting. She didn't protest when you suggested that she wear certain outfits taken from your wardrobe, and, as for you, you showed no signs of offense when she suggested that you shorten the length of your skirts.

She's highly sensitive to criticism and knows how to effectively express her frustrations. She can be rebellious and vengeful, and she coldly accepts our compliments, meant to encourage her personal improvement, as if she were rejecting any possibility of change. Though she's often hesitant and slow to understand our instructions, we succeeded in teaching her how to correctly wield a fork and knife. The proper usage of certain household objects escapes her completely, and she demonstrates insurmountable difficulties in carrying out the most elementary (from our perspective) of tasks, like opening a can or tying her shoes. When she encounters a problem, be it technical or intellectual, her face tightens and her mind closes itself obstinately to the minimal amount of reflection needed for a solution. Conscious of the impediments and diverse obstacles that limit her daily activities to the most boring and banal of tasks, we don't trust her with any responsibilities that lie beyond the scope of her abilities. Her intelligence is mediocre, but her memory is infallible. She can recite by heart the shopping lists we put her in charge of, and she easily identifies the country roads we sometimes drive along to escape the monotony of Sundays and bank holidays. She isn't incapable of a certain kind of slyness, and we suspect she has a natural and irresistible propensity for lying. On several occasions, she's neglected to give us the change from a shopping trip, and she's committed small acts of larceny that we prefer to close our eyes to, fearing that she might dramatically leave the house faced with even a minor accusation. She hates to be at fault and won't tolerate suggestions for personal improvement. Content with her imperfect syntax and limited vocabulary to crudely express her needs and wishes, she sees no value in education, and her daily reading is limited to flipping through the pages of the TV guide. She sometimes gets out of bed in the middle of the afternoon and, in defiance of all modesty, struts through the living room, completely naked or in multicolored underwear, while we stare helplessly on, incapable of taking our eyes off her tanned, perfectly shaped body. We abstain from saying her name, fearing that we might mispronounce it, and to avoid humiliating her, we're careful to avoid difficult subjects that would require the use of complicated words while in her

presence. She refuses to let herself give in to pity and seems to
exist in a never-ending present constrained only by the finite
number of her appetites. Her sense of humor is frighteningly
deficient, but her sexual vitality knows no bounds. Incapable of
taking the initiative in helping with the management of daily
chores, she's developed a supernatural inventiveness in her hunt
for pleasure and distraction. She's experienced and driven, and
the sight of her naked body makes us feel like flawed, discount
toys. She's awakened in us repressed pains and unsuspected pas-
sions. Her gaze is devoid of emotion, we've never seen a hint of
fear or contempt in her eyes, and when we hear the ringing of
her laughter, paired with the sight of her crooked, rotten teeth,
we tremble like small children caught in the act.

We've reduced the number of our outings and, unwilling to tolerate the untimely and invasive presence of the workers, neglected the roof's overdue repairs. She's extinguished our taste for
travel and taught us to view the world without emotion. Thanks
to her, we've rediscovered our taste for life and have put a stop
to our unrestrained consumption of antidepressants. Although I
strongly disapprove of a girl her age going alone to a nightclub,
when she asks me for the car keys, I give in immediately to her
demand, feeling powerless to refuse her. In a certain sense, it's
her who's adopted us. She never speaks of her past and has never
used the phone to call a parent or a friend. Reclusive and sulky,
she's never expressed any desires beyond being allowed to eat to
contentment and be left in peace. We've given up once and for
all on trying to learn her country of origin, satisfying ourselves
with the rare and often contradictory pieces of information
she agrees to share with us. She immediately had an instinctive
knowledge of our most secret longings, and she taught us how to
liberate ourselves from the prejudices and burdens forged in us
by past experiences. When she fell pregnant, you never stooped
so low as to insinuate that I might be the father, and together

we had to handle her recurring panic attacks and fits of anger during the gestation. After her departure one week after the delivery, as sudden as it was unexplained, we felt no bitterness toward her and surrounded the child with the tenderest of affections. He calls you mama and provides you with the purest joy life has ever shown you.

Sunday Afternoon

THE CONVERSATION HAS started back up, along with the soft scraping of forks and knives, and she sits before a plate of roast, accompanied by lukewarm potatoes, that she absorbs without appetite. No matter how bad she might have wanted to, she was unable to refuse the invitation, and now, too tired or intimidated to lock eyes with the faces surrounding her, she smiles politely and vacantly at everything while straining to conceal the repugnance she feels at the smell of cold ash drifting out of the fireplace and the sight of flypaper hanging above the table. Conscious of the eyes pointed in her direction, she consumes cold meat and potatoes with the affected and deliberate slowness that has always been one of her defining characteristics. Just moments before, she was standing in her red silk dress, hesitant, discomfited, and somewhat dazed, anticipating the humiliation she would feel as they led her to her designated place at the table, thinking about how disastrous a mistake it was to have come here among these people who seemed so ecstatic to see her. The house is surrounded by corn and situated at the edge of a freshly paved road, on which the rare cars that pass go speeding briskly by. From afar, the house seems imposing, or it at least imposes the idea of a certain majesty and isolated ruggedness, but up close it looks more like an unexceptional outbuilding, hastily built with cheap, substandard materials. She knows all of the house's rooms, certain ones, like the living room, bathroom, and the blue upstairs bedroom, she even knows quite intimately, while others remain mostly a mystery to her. One day, when no one else was there, she briefly inspected every room in the house, driven by curiosity as much as a secret suspicion that she wasn't actually there alone. Throughout the years she spent here, she remembers having experienced a wide spectrum of emotions, ranging from boredom to joy, the one common factor among them all being that they left no lasting effect on her, as if they had all been felt in a painful and somehow degrading dream from which she couldn't escape. There's no river in the surrounding area, an isolated nightclub, frequented by the idle inhabitants from the neighboring villages, is the only nearby attraction. They ask for news about her parents, her brothers, they force intrusive, superficial questions on her to which she mechanically and unresistingly responds, and she considers how inappropriate it would be to reveal her true thoughts in the unevenly and unfashionably furnished living room. She came by coach to the nearest village and then walked three kilometers through a suffocating heat from the bus station to her family-in-law's house. They casually inquire about her health and asthma without listening to her responses, they compliment her on her low-cut red dress but also express surprise, with an undertone of self-righteous indignation, that she didn't think to bring something to cover her shoulders from the sun. Nothing about her has changed, and she will undoubtedly always have her distant, reticent manner of behaving. She's twenty-seven years old, and she's a widow. She teaches either English or German in the technical high school of an industrial city, and her students, not much younger than she is, view her with a mixture of respect and disbelief. Although she never complained about it, she seemed perpetually bored as a child, showing indifference toward companionship and pushing away with a glare any adult who thought they could bring her out of her shell by feigning a kind of complicity with her. She learned how to walk relatively late, but spent most of her childhood sitting down. She had no close friends and never had any interest in the intimate secrets and passionate bonds that make up adolescence. Before reaching thirteen, her body had developed, and she was already taller than most adult women, but she still childishly refused to leave her bedroom for anything other than meals. She's unfriendly, and her colleagues, after having debated their chances of sleeping with her, never approach her without a certain reluctance. She's never had to bargain to get what she wants and has never made an effort to be conciliatory. On Sundays in winter, her slender, black silhouette can be made out on the vast gray beach near her city, her presence on Earth seeming to be cursed by erosion. She passes by strolling couples to whom she pays no attention, and with her face turned toward the pale, intensely green ocean, she experiences of a form of misery that she makes no effort to escape. She could walk for hours on the fringe of the hard, moist sand, barefoot despite the cold, without feeling any need to stop; making no effort to give her thoughts precise boundaries, she wouldn't pretend to know either who she is or where she's going, and should she be requested to reveal her identity after being stopped on a village square after nightfall, she would give only a thin smile in response. She lives in a two-room apartment on the top floor of a tower-like building with a view of the port, where she likes to stay shut away before and after work, unoccupied and inattentive, with the sound of the radio set to its lowest level. Here, she has everything necessary for her comfort and survival. Nothing is missing, and she considers it a stroke of luck and even a luxury to lead such a tranquil life in her neutral setting, where every object has a precise purpose and nothing is superfluous. Although she hasn't tried to give the place any particular imprint or personal touch, she never receives visits from friends or family, fearing that it would cause a climactic variation in her environment that would render it suddenly hostile and inhabitable. Once every week, she meets a temporary lover in a hotel room, sometimes married, sometimes single, after having agreed on a time and place in a brief, sometimes sarcastic, conversation over the telephone. Before each encounter, she visualizes a detail of the man's anatomy or imagines an unexpected movement that she could make to destabilize his desire, placing herself halfway between attraction and disgust in the eyes of this man with whom she will share no more than one or two hours of her life. She's always given off an impression of not being an integral part of the contemporary world. She's never the first one to speak, and she never talks about her despair or misfortune in the presence of strangers. She's hard to impress, and she doesn't try to arouse jealousy, desire, or admiration in others, but on certain mornings, like today's, she likes to dress with a certain ostentation. She has no social ambitions and does everything imprecisely, whether it's giving directions to a stranger in the street, recalling the name of a black and white film, or remembering what size clothes she wears. The heat, the heavy boredom, and the feeling of her incapacity to understand what these people expect exhaust her. The sideways glances still watch her expectantly, on the lookout for some reaction. The pace of the questioning has slowed down and, under the effects of impatience and disappointment, their faces seem to have hardened and congealed into expressions of incomprehension. They want her to be more talkative, more intensely present. Any signs of life seem to have left her pale and worried face, and, as if moving through a painful, demeaning, and endless dream, she feels as if she's lost all volition. She knows she should be more communicative, or at least more sentimental. In vain, she tries to conjure up a memory and connect it to the atmosphere and mood of the evening, but the fear of exposing her emotions bridles any attempt to express herself sincerely. She never reflects on her past, and her dreams mean nothing to her. Taking advantage of a sudden letup in conversation while dessert is being served, a voice addresses her from across the table. Does this have to come at the precise moment when, realizing how much of an outsider she is here, she feels as if she's on the verge of succumbing to her fatigue? He speaks in a trembling and reedy voice, with an intolerable slowness that forces her to be immersed in each word before she can seize the meaning of the sentences struggling to reach her. The slowness is infuriating and might destroy her on the spot, but her attention is fortunately diverted by the hands of the person sitting to her right, and because of these hands, she can find no reason to let herself be affected by the words she's now hearing. These long, skinny hands, clearly those of an adolescent, but whose face she doesn't care to meet, tap on the table while spinning the shimmering blade of a silver knife above the tablecloth, and she cannot look away from them, condemned to watch them with a sort of fervor or exalted distress. These are the tireless and finely crafted hands of a weak, inconsequential boy, precise hands made for the subtle movements required for card tricks but useless for heavy labor or the handling of a shovel. These hands make her feel an excessive, anxious, and painful affection for the boy manipulating them with an almost pathological agility, as if they functioned independently of his body and his only responsibility was to watch them dance. Faced with these frenzied, burning hands, she feels a brutal, insatiable nostalgia. Where could he be right now, the man who should be at her side, talkative and visible, cheerful and discretely compliant, working so that everyone could be happy on a day like today? she wonders, feverish with heat and thirst. He died of cardiac arrest, and she never felt anything more for him than a silent, rarely expressed attraction, that some might have judged deliberately austere. As if they'd taken over every last bit of her intelligence and reasoning, the hands prevent her from focusing on the speaker's words, these intoxicating and tireless hands have rendered her deaf and blind, unintelligible to herself. What would become of her should she suddenly transform into the blade of the knife, stripped of all volition and power, reduced to spinning and dancing with small, crisp movements between the agile fingers, controlled with the precision of a skilled equestrian? What would happen to me if I stopped being myself and became the nimble knife in this young man's hands? She can see herself again, locked in a phone booth to hide her tears, her body folded in two by the twisting pain in her stomach, an excavator drilling into her body. She again sees herself bedridden, shriveled up into herself, her hair filthy. She sees herself again in different moods, the majority demonstrating her inability to connect to reality using the methods so naturally executed by everyone else since the dawn of time. She would have been better off remaining a fetus. She could have transfigured herself into a corpse if the image of her emaciated body in the mirror hadn't made her vomit. She's alive and focused, her memory is faultless. She knows that she's indivisible and deserving, images from the past stream through her mind with the speed of the wind she felt earlier that day, toward the end of the afternoon. She views her life as a stone that refuses to be shattered by regret. The conversation has extinguished itself of its own accord, the hands have fallen still in response to some mysterious, unseen signal. They sit calmly, abandoned and fragile. It's too late to return home by bus, and now that it's night and the house has fallen silent, she stretches out naked in a spacious bed, shining in the darkness of a room prepared specifically for her, thinking she can hear the wind rustling through the cornfields.

Intimacy

THE PHOTO'S QUALITY is wanting, the lighting in which you pose is raw and unflattering. I don't know who took it, I found it by accident in one of those ancient iron boxes where you kept all kinds of useless things that you just had to hold on to, driven by an attachment as naïve as it was superstitious to a past you weren't particularly fond of. At first glance, it's a rather banal, maybe even botched, photo of you in a neon-lit bathroom, and each time I see it, I experience a sharp pain that's impossible to locate. It's clearly you, although I've never seen the expression you're making, and I experience an unhealthy attraction looking at you like this, framed under the dirty, yellow light at the end of the evening. The photo's here, beneath my eyes, and the preciseness with which it represents you and everything that it divulges about the situation in which you found yourself at that exact moment overwhelm me with the force of a meteoric revelation. The photo reveals everything, but it's your face that stands out more than anything else, your beautiful face, illuminated by intensity and showing the exhaustion felt by someone naked and desperate, your eyes half-closed against the strong light, reflected violently by the bathroom tiles, being projected by the camera. The photo reveals everything, and although it's somewhat blurry, as if the photographer was trembling at the moment he took it, it distorts no detail of your exposed body. The legs, the stomach, the breasts, the hand holding the nearly finished cigarette and the face turned toward the ceiling, everything is captured with an agonizing exactitude. These young girl's legs that I so often kissed, this stomach, these breasts and knees and every other detail shown off by your nakedness, I examine them all with an obsessive acuity. Did the photographer ask you to raise yourself up a little out of the bathwater to expose your cute, little breasts, wet and shiny from the water, the nipples hard and brown? Was he likewise trying to satisfy his lustful curiosity by asking you to lift your ass up in order to bring your wet pussy to the surface of the water? There's no doubt that the photographer was a man; a lover, a boyfriend, a fleeting stranger fished out of a nightclub, I'll never know, and truth be told, I don't care to know. He was there, this man, focusing on your body from behind the lens of his camera, and you gave in to his instructions with a tender passivity and a perfect understanding of what was necessary to make the photo a success, unless it was in fact you who suggested, for reasons unknown to me, this late-night photo shoot in the miniature bathroom saturated with steam and cigarette smoke, perhaps because he'd demonstrated remarkable talent while making love to you and you'd experienced afterward, along with a profound and idiotic appreciation, a determination to prove to yourself that it was worth the struggle to go on living and to immortalize this moment in which you felt so close to bliss. Did you have even the slightest idea of how beautiful you were in that moment? Were you high, were you in love? Perhaps you were both at the same time, and the two sensations had become inseparable in your mind, bonded together in a way I'll never be capable of understanding. One thing is certain, you show the particular exhaustion that only sex can bring about, that benign exhaustion that lasts and lasts and refuses to fade until the first signs of morning. The light hurts your eyes, and it looks as if you were sleeping, but nothing could be further from the truth. You're twenty-seven years old, you're not happy, and you give in with a feverish indulgence to every new experience that comes your way, and your face, in this moment of uncertainty, reveals a strange mixture of unreality, disorientation, and fear, your face reveals an absolute and morbid acquiescence, directed calmly at yourself toward the interior area in which lurks your despair, an acquiescence not derived from resignation or passivity but from an understanding, finally received, finally attained, of why you're there. The photo is blurry and seems botched, but it wouldn't be so perfect and so disturbing if it didn't seem a little botched because of the blur. Was the photographer, he as well, so horny or so high that he couldn't hold the camera steady? It's not difficult for me to reconstruct your journey back here to Rue Wievorka, and the images thrash about violently inside my head as I replay every sequence of your evening together. You met him in a train station or fished him from the dark, icy waters of a nightclub infested by shady and perverted men who ogled you obsessively, and it wasn't long before the two of you had filled each other with a ravenous desire that screamed for immediate satisfaction. Everything is silent and damp in the bathroom, a small cylinder of warm ash falls in slow motion into the water, and you're making no attempt to erase the unwanted aspects of your dissolute life, led in contempt of your morals and your conviction that somewhere on Earth the possibility of happiness must exist. He spread your legs, he ejaculated into your mouth and anus, he did a variety of things you can't remember, he got, in the end, everything he'd wanted out of you. You were passionate and yielding, you were slow-burning and explosive like a volcano, and you made yourself, in the space of a night, the impeccable instrument of his pleasure, the little providential slut picked up one freezing-to-death evening; a skilled predator, he knew what was in store for him the second he saw you coming in his direction toward the bar. He was on your trail, and you were situated, as needed, within the crosshairs of his scope, and now he stands leaning over the bathtub, perched on a stool or a step ladder, and you stare at the lens as if it were at once the most desirable and most repulsive thing in the world, while everything surrounding

you is formless and wet, and ashes lie scattered throughout the
water clinging to pieces of foam, driven in a peaceful Brownian
motion toward their uncertain fate. And so, I think to myself,
this man whose face is hidden behind the camera, he must have
fucked you for the duration of the night, demonstrating a rare
sexual perfectionism and a sophisticated understanding of how
to push you inexorably toward orgasm, and under such circumstances you would, of course, feel a little in love, because there
would be nothing outrageous or even absurd about falling a little
in love with a man who scoops you up out of the street and fucks
you professionally, as if you were both a queen and whore, for
the duration of the night, and in the confined space of the blue
and yellow bathroom, you do in fact feel a little like a queen
and a little like a whore, and you can think of nothing more
satisfying than holding out your delicate face to the stranger
in a sign of appreciation or in desperate acquiescence to that
which was so close to happening but which, thank God, didn't
happen, let's call it a miracle of your ambiguous, desperate, vic-
timized smile in the blue and yellow bathroom, where all your
senses feel heightened and where whatever innocence that still
exists within you is close to evaporating. You're vulnerable, and
you have the body of a malnourished young girl or a repentant
junkie, and it feels like a cold, impersonal poem to find yourself
in this situation, conscious of the happiness missing in your
life, floating momentarily in this emptiness and silence, while
at the same time, you appear extremely strong and immensely
proud, and I tell myself that the innocence still residing inside
you hasn't yet died.

It's been three years since we've seen each other, and I now find
myself in the same nightclub as you, trapped uncomfortably
near the bar, not knowing why I'm here. I've changed my daily
routines and avoided with a cautious consistency any place where
I'm likely to see you, fearing that I might collapse the moment

I meet your eyes. It's been weeks since I've spoken to anyone, since I've felt capable of creating the circumstances suitable for an intimate, or even constructive, conversation with a member of the opposite sex. You don't recognize me, which is in no way surprising, I'm wearing dark sunglasses, and my figure has considerably thickened; living exclusively on beer, chocolate bars, and medication, I've put on a pile of kilograms, and flesh has accumulated around my body like dirt at a construction site. In a voice altered by the combined effects of fatigue and sedatives, I offer you a cigarette, and it's obvious you still don't recognize me, and I feel relieved at the thought that I'm nothing more to you than an obscure memory that my physical presence is incapable of recalling. And you, you're still as thin as always, the pregnancies haven't deformed your body in the least. Your piercing, childish laugh, emitted like a brief, disenchanting note with a tinge of fatalism, still wreaks the same havoc on my soul. You're wearing dark turquoise pants, a bright red hooded jacket, and you still seem stuck in a state of perpetual adolescence. You're thirty years old, you're perfect, and you move through this world like a chimerical child raised by idealistic parents who failed to instill in you the principles of life required to follow the paths of happiness and conformity, and in this seedy nightclub, infested by insidious strangers and shifty men, you sway and tilt among the circles of light like a composite fantasy created from the imagination of every last man on Earth. You're limpid and poignant, and your face is sometimes so revealing that I can watch the exact progression of the thoughts through your head, just as I could on that catastrophic day when you announced, with a smile on your lips, that you were leaving me. Once again, you're desperately and obviously available, and you finally let yourself be overtaken by some guy who emerges suddenly out of the shadows and who has no doubt been watching you for a good deal of time now. So alone again, sitting on my bed, I take out the photo, stolen on the day I realized we were finished forever and which I've conserved like a relic, a talisman, evidence of my suffering stored between two pages of a book. The photo's in my trembling hand, it's the photo that makes me suffer so much, I know that it's pathetic to suffer like I do because of a photo, the photo of you, your face in the steam, euphoric, ecstatic even, or maybe just high. I'm looking at it again, with an excruciating lust that's impossible to satisfy, I wish it didn't exist, but I don't have the strength to ignore it, and I know that I could never bring myself to destroy it.

SÉBASTIEN BREBEL was born in 1971 in Argenteuil, France, and now lives in Nantes, where he teaches philosophy. He is the author of three novels, available in English from Dalkey Archive Press: *Villa Bunker* (2013), *Francis Bacon's Armchair* (2016), and *A Perfect Disharmony* (2017).

JESSE ANDERSON is a literary translator and writer from Olympia, Washington. His fiction and poetry have appeared in various literary journals and online.

MICHAL AJVAZ, *The Golden Age.*
The Other City.
PIERRE ALBERT-BIROT, *Grabinoulor.*
YUZ ALESHKOVSKY, *Kangaroo.*
FELIPE ALFAU, *Chromos.*
Locos.
JOE AMATO, *Samuel Taylor's Last Night.*
IVAN ÂNGELO, *The Celebration.*
The Tower of Glass.
ANTÓNIO LOBO ANTUNES, *Knowledge of Hell.*
The Splendor of Portugal.
ALAIN ARIAS-MISSON, *Theatre of Incest.*
JOHN ASHBERY & JAMES SCHUYLER, *A Nest of Ninnies.*
ROBERT ASHLEY, *Perfect Lives.*
GABRIELA AVIGUR-ROTEM, *Heatwave and Crazy Birds.*
DJUNA BARNES, *Ladies Almanack.*
Ryder.
JOHN BARTH, *Letters.*
Sabbatical.
DONALD BARTHELME, *The King.*
Paradise.
SVETISLAV BASARA, *Chinese Letter.*
MIQUEL BAUÇÀ, *The Siege in the Room.*
RENÉ BELLETTO, *Dying.*
MAREK BIENCZYK, *Transparency.*
ANDREI BITOV, *Pushkin House.*
ANDREJ BLATNIK, *You Do Understand.*
Law of Desire.
LOUIS PAUL BOON, *Chapel Road.*
My Little War.
Summer in Termuren.
ROGER BOYLAN, *Killoyle.*
IGNÁCIO DE LOYOLA BRANDÃO, *Anonymous Celebrity.*
Zero.
BONNIE BREMSER, *Troia: Mexican Memoirs.*
CHRISTINE BROOKE-ROSE, *Amalgamemnon.*
BRIGID BROPHY, *In Transit.*
The Prancing Novelist.

GERALD L. BRUNS, *Modern Poetry and the Idea of Language.*
GABRIELLE BURTON, *Heartbreak Hotel.*
MICHEL BUTOR, *Degrees.*
Mobile.
G. CABRERA INFANTE, *Infante's Inferno.*
Three Trapped Tigers.
JULIETA CAMPOS, *The Fear of Losing Eurydice.*
ANNE CARSON, *Eros the Bittersweet.*
ORLY CASTEL-BLOOM, *Dolly City.*
LOUIS-FERDINAND CÉLINE, *North.*
Conversations with Professor Y.
London Bridge.
MARIE CHAIX, *The Laurels of Lake Constance.*
HUGO CHARTERIS, *The Tide Is Right.*
ERIC CHEVILLARD, *Demolishing Nisard.*
The Author and Me.
MARC CHOLODENKO, *Mordechai Schamz.*
JOSHUA COHEN, *Witz.*
EMILY HOLMES COLEMAN, *The Shutter of Snow.*
ERIC CHEVILLARD, *The Author and Me.*
ROBERT COOVER, *A Night at the Movies.*
STANLEY CRAWFORD, *Log of the S.S. The Mrs Unguentine.*
Some Instructions to My Wife.
RENÉ CREVEL, *Putting My Foot in It.*
RALPH CUSACK, *Cadenza.*
NICHOLAS DELBANCO, *Sherbrookes.*
The Count of Concord.
NIGEL DENNIS, *Cards of Identity.*
PETER DIMOCK, *A Short Rhetoric for Leaving the Family.*
ARIEL DORFMAN, *Konfidenz.*
COLEMAN DOWELL, *Island People.*
Too Much Flesh and Jabez.
ARKADII DRAGOMOSHCHENKO, *Dust.*
RIKKI DUCORNET, *Phosphor in Dreamland.*
The Complete Butcher's Tales.

RIKKI DUCORNET (cont.), *The Jade Cabinet*.
The Fountains of Neptune.
WILLIAM EASTLAKE, *The Bamboo Bed*.
Castle Keep.
Lyric of the Circle Heart.
JEAN ECHENOZ, *Chopin's Move*.
STANLEY ELKIN, *A Bad Man*.
Criers and Kibitzers, Kibitzers and Criers.
The Dick Gibson Show.
The Franchiser.
The Living End.
Mrs. Ted Bliss.
FRANÇOIS EMMANUEL, *Invitation to a Voyage*.
PAUL EMOND, *The Dance of a Sham*.
SALVADOR ESPRIU, *Ariadne in the Grotesque Labyrinth*.
LESLIE A. FIEDLER, *Love and Death in the American Novel*.
JUAN FILLOY, *Op Oloop*.
ANDY FITCH, *Pop Poetics*.
GUSTAVE FLAUBERT, *Bouvard and Pécuchet*.
KASS FLEISHER, *Talking out of School*.
JON FOSSE, *Aliss at the Fire*.
Melancholy.
FORD MADOX FORD, *The March of Literature*.
MAX FRISCH, *I'm Not Stiller*.
Man in the Holocene.
CARLOS FUENTES, *Christopher Unborn*.
Distant Relations.
Terra Nostra.
Where the Air Is Clear.
TAKEHIKO FUKUNAGA, *Flowers of Grass*.
WILLIAM GADDIS, JR., *The Recognitions*.
JANICE GALLOWAY, *Foreign Parts*.
The Trick Is to Keep Breathing.
WILLIAM H. GASS, *Life Sentences*.
The Tunnel.
The World Within the Word.
Willie Masters' Lonesome Wife.
GÉRARD GAVARRY, *Hoppla! 1 2 3*.

ETIENNE GILSON, *The Arts of the Beautiful*.
Forms and Substances in the Arts.
C. S. GISCOMBE, *Giscome Road*.
Here.
DOUGLAS GLOVER, *Bad News of the Heart*.
WITOLD GOMBROWICZ, *A Kind of Testament*.
PAULO EMÍLIO SALES GOMES, *P's Three Women*.
GEORGI GOSPODINOV, *Natural Novel*.
JUAN GOYTISOLO, *Count Julian*.
Juan the Landless.
Makbara.
Marks of Identity.
HENRY GREEN, *Blindness*.
Concluding.
Doting.
Nothing.
JACK GREEN, *Fire the Bastards!*
JIŘÍ GRUŠA, *The Questionnaire*.
MELA HARTWIG, *Am I a Redundant Human Being?*
JOHN HAWKES, *The Passion Artist*.
Whistlejacket.
ELIZABETH HEIGHWAY, ED., *Contemporary Georgian Fiction*.
AIDAN HIGGINS, *Balcony of Europe*.
Blind Man's Bluff.
Bornholm Night-Ferry.
Langrishe, Go Down.
Scenes from a Receding Past.
KEIZO HINO, *Isle of Dreams*.
KAZUSHI HOSAKA, *Plainsong*.
ALDOUS HUXLEY, *Antic Hay*.
Point Counter Point.
Those Barren Leaves.
Time Must Have a Stop.
NAOYUKI II, *The Shadow of a Blue Cat*.
DRAGO JANČAR, *The Tree with No Name*.
MIKHEIL JAVAKHISHVILI, *Kvachi*.
GERT JONKE, *The Distant Sound*.
Homage to Czerny.
The System of Vienna.

JACQUES JOUET, *Mountain R.*
Savage.
Upstaged.
MIEKO KANAI, *The Word Book.*
YORAM KANIUK, *Life on Sandpaper.*
ZURAB KARUMIDZE, *Dagny.*
JOHN KELLY, *From Out of the City.*
HUGH KENNER, *Flaubert, Joyce and Beckett: The Stoic Comedians.*
Joyce's Voices.
DANILO KIŠ, *The Attic.*
The Lute and the Scars.
Psalm 44.
A Tomb for Boris Davidovich.
ANITA KONKKA, *A Fool's Paradise.*
GEORGE KONRÁD, *The City Builder.*
TADEUSZ KONWICKI, *A Minor Apocalypse.*
The Polish Complex.
ANNA KORDZAIA-SAMADASHVILI, *Me, Margarita.*
MENIS KOUMANDAREAS, *Koula.*
ELAINE KRAF, *The Princess of 72nd Street.*
JIM KRUSOE, *Iceland.*
AYSE KULIN, *Farewell: A Mansion in Occupied Istanbul.*
EMILIO LASCANO TEGUI, *On Elegance While Sleeping.*
ERIC LAURRENT, *Do Not Touch.*
VIOLETTE LEDUC, *La Bâtarde.*
EDOUARD LEVÉ, *Autoportrait.*
Newspaper.
Suicide.
Works.
MARIO LEVI, *Istanbul Was a Fairy Tale.*
DEBORAH LEVY, *Billy and Girl.*
JOSÉ LEZAMA LIMA, *Paradiso.*
ROSA LIKSOM, *Dark Paradise.*
OSMAN LINS, *Avalovara.*
The Queen of the Prisons of Greece.
FLORIAN LIPUŠ, *The Errors of Young Tjaž.*
GORDON LISH, *Peru.*
ALF MACLOCHLAINN, *Out of Focus.*
Past Habitual.

The Corpus in the Library.
RON LOEWINSOHN, *Magnetic Field(s).*
YURI LOTMAN, *Non-Memoirs.*
D. KEITH MANO, *Take Five.*
MINA LOY, *Stories and Essays of Mina Loy.*
MICHELINE AHARONIAN MARCOM, *A Brief History of Yes.*
The Mirror in the Well.
BEN MARCUS, *The Age of Wire and String.*
WALLACE MARKFIELD, *Teitlebaum's Window.*
DAVID MARKSON, *Reader's Block.*
Wittgenstein's Mistress.
CAROLE MASO, *AVA.*
HISAKI MATSUURA, *Triangle.*
LADISLAV MATEJKA & KRYSTYNA POMORSKA, EDS., *Readings in Russian Poetics: Formalist & Structuralist Views.*
HARRY MATHEWS, *Cigarettes.*
The Conversions.
The Human Country.
The Journalist.
My Life in CIA.
Singular Pleasures.
The Sinking of the Odradek.
Stadium.
Tlooth.
HISAKI MATSUURA, *Triangle.*
DONAL MCLAUGHLIN, *beheading the virgin mary, and other stories.*
JOSEPH MCELROY, *Night Soul and Other Stories.*
ABDELWAHAB MEDDEB, *Talismano.*
GERHARD MEIER, *Isle of the Dead.*
HERMAN MELVILLE, *The Confidence-Man.*
AMANDA MICHALOPOULOU, *I'd Like.*
STEVEN MILLHAUSER, *The Barnum Museum.*
In the Penny Arcade.
RALPH J. MILLS, JR., *Essays on Poetry.*
MOMUS, *The Book of Jokes.*
CHRISTINE MONTALBETTI, *The Origin of Man.*
Western.

NICHOLAS MOSLEY, *Accident.*
Assassins.
Catastrophe Practice.
A Garden of Trees.
Hopeful Monsters.
Imago Bird.
Inventing God.
Look at the Dark.
Metamorphosis.
Natalie Natalia.
Serpent.
WARREN MOTTE, *Fables of the Novel: French Fiction since 1990.*
Fiction Now: The French Novel in the 21st Century.
Mirror Gazing.
Oulipo: A Primer of Potential Literature.
GERALD MURNANE, *Barley Patch.*
Inland.
YVES NAVARRE, *Our Share of Time.*
Sweet Tooth.
DOROTHY NELSON, *In Night's City.*
Tar and Feathers.
ESHKOL NEVO, *Homesick.*
WILFRIDO D. NOLLEDO, *But for the Lovers.*
BORIS A. NOVAK, *The Master of Insomnia.*
FLANN O'BRIEN, *At Swim-Two-Birds.*
The Best of Myles.
The Dalkey Archive.
The Hard Life.
The Poor Mouth.
The Third Policeman.
CLAUDE OLLIER, *The Mise-en-Scène.*
Wert and the Life Without End.
PATRIK OUŘEDNÍK, *Europeana.*
The Opportune Moment, 1855.
BORIS PAHOR, *Necropolis.*
FERNANDO DEL PASO, *News from the Empire.*
Palinuro of Mexico.
ROBERT PINGET, *The Inquisitory.*
Mahu or The Material.
Trio.
MANUEL PUIG, *Betrayed by Rita Hayworth.*

The Buenos Aires Affair.
Heartbreak Tango.
RAYMOND QUENEAU, *The Last Days.*
Odile.
Pierrot Mon Ami.
Saint Glinglin.
ANN QUIN, *Berg.*
Passages.
Three.
Tripticks.
ISHMAEL REED, *The Free-Lance Pallbearers.*
The Last Days of Louisiana Red.
Ishmael Reed: The Plays.
Juice!
The Terrible Threes.
The Terrible Twos.
Yellow Back Radio Broke-Down.
JASIA REICHARDT, *15 Journeys Warsaw to London.*
JOÃO UBALDO RIBEIRO, *House of the Fortunate Buddhas.*
JEAN RICARDOU, *Place Names.*
RAINER MARIA RILKE,
The Notebooks of Malte Laurids Brigge.
JULIÁN RÍOS, *The House of Ulysses.*
Larva: A Midsummer Night's Babel.
Poundemonium.
ALAIN ROBBE-GRILLET, *Project for a Revolution in New York.*
A Sentimental Novel.
AUGUSTO ROA BASTOS, *I the Supreme.*
DANIËL ROBBERECHTS, *Arriving in Avignon.*
JEAN ROLIN, *The Explosion of the Radiator Hose.*
OLIVIER ROLIN, *Hotel Crystal.*
ALIX CLEO ROUBAUD, *Alix's Journal.*
JACQUES ROUBAUD, *The Form of a City Changes Faster, Alas, Than the Human Heart.*
The Great Fire of London.
Hortense in Exile.
Hortense Is Abducted.
Mathematics: The Plurality of Worlds of Lewis.
Some Thing Black.

RAYMOND ROUSSEL, *Impressions of Africa.*

VEDRANA RUDAN, *Night.*

PABLO M. RUIZ, *Four Cold Chapters on the Possibility of Literature.*

GERMAN SADULAEV, *The Maya Pill.*

TOMAŽ ŠALAMUN, *Soy Realidad.*

LYDIE SALVAYRE, *The Company of Ghosts.*
The Lecture.
The Power of Flies.

LUIS RAFAEL SÁNCHEZ, *Macho Camacho's Beat.*

SEVERO SARDUY, *Cobra & Maitreya.*

NATHALIE SARRAUTE, *Do You Hear Them?*
Martereau.
The Planetarium.

STIG SÆTERBAKKEN, *Siamese.*
Self-Control.
Through the Night.

ARNO SCHMIDT, *Collected Novellas.*
Collected Stories.
Nobodaddy's Children.
Two Novels.

ASAF SCHURR, *Motti.*

GAIL SCOTT, *My Paris.*

DAMION SEARLS, *What We Were Doing and Where We Were Going.*

JUNE AKERS SEESE, *Is This What Other Women Feel Too?*

BERNARD SHARE, *Inish.*
Transit.

VIKTOR SHKLOVSKY, *Bowstring.*
Literature and Cinematography.
Theory of Prose.
Third Factory.
Zoo, or Letters Not about Love.

PIERRE SINIAC, *The Collaborators.*

KJERSTI A. SKOMSVOLD, *The Faster I Walk, the Smaller I Am.*

JOSEF ŠKVORECKÝ, *The Engineer of Human Souls.*

GILBERT SORRENTINO, *Aberration of Starlight.*
Blue Pastoral.
Crystal Vision.

Imaginative Qualities of Actual Things.
Mulligan Stew. Red the Fiend.
Steelwork.
Under the Shadow.

MARKO SOSIČ, *Ballerina, Ballerina.*

ANDRZEJ STASIUK, *Dukla.*
Fado.

GERTRUDE STEIN, *The Making of Americans.*
A Novel of Thank You.

LARS SVENDSEN, *A Philosophy of Evil.*

PIOTR SZEWC, *Annihilation.*

GONÇALO M. TAVARES, *A Man: Klaus Klump.*
Jerusalem.
Learning to Pray in the Age of Technique.

LUCIAN DAN TEODOROVICI, *Our Circus Presents...*

NIKANOR TERATOLOGEN, *Assisted Living.*

STEFAN THEMERSON, *Hobson's Island.*
The Mystery of the Sardine.
Tom Harris.

TAEKO TOMIOKA, *Building Waves.*

JOHN TOOMEY, *Sleepwalker.*

DUMITRU TSEPENEAG, *Hotel Europa.*
The Necessary Marriage.
Pigeon Post.
Vain Art of the Fugue.

ESTHER TUSQUETS, *Stranded.*

DUBRAVKA UGRESIC, *Lend Me Your Character.*
Thank You for Not Reading.

TOR ULVEN, *Replacement.*

MATI UNT, *Brecht at Night.*
Diary of a Blood Donor.
Things in the Night.

ÁLVARO URIBE & OLIVIA SEARS, EDS., *Best of Contemporary Mexican Fiction.*

ELOY URROZ, *Friction.*
The Obstacles.

LUISA VALENZUELA, *Dark Desires and the Others.*
He Who Searches.

PAUL VERHAEGHEN, *Omega Minor.*

BORIS VIAN, *Heartsnatcher.*

LLORENÇ VILLALONGA, *The Dolls' Room.*

TOOMAS VINT, *An Unending Landscape.*

ORNELA VORPSI, *The Country Where No One Ever Dies.*

AUSTRYN WAINHOUSE, *Hedyphagetica.*

CURTIS WHITE, *America's Magic Mountain.*
The Idea of Home.
Memories of My Father Watching TV.
Requiem.

DIANE WILLIAMS,
Excitability: Selected Stories.
Romancer Erector.

DOUGLAS WOOLF, *Wall to Wall.*
Ya! & John-Juan.

JAY WRIGHT, *Polynomials and Pollen.*
The Presentable Art of Reading Absence.

PHILIP WYLIE, *Generation of Vipers.*

MARGUERITE YOUNG, *Angel in the Forest.*
Miss MacIntosh, My Darling.

REYOUNG, *Unbabbling.*

VLADO ŽABOT, *The Succubus.*

ZORAN ŽIVKOVIĆ , *Hidden Camera.*

LOUIS ZUKOFSKY, *Collected Fiction.*

VITOMIL ZUPAN, *Minuet for Guitar.*

SCOTT ZWIREN, *God Head.*

AND MORE . . .